OATHBREAKER

THE KNIGHT'S TALE | Book 1

BY COLIN MCCOMB

See also the Monumental Works Group
www.monumentalworksgroup.com

Cover art created and copyright © 2011 by Stone Perales
www.stonewurks.com

Graphic design by Don Strandell
www.donstrandell.com

Electronic formatting by Guido Henkel
www.guidohenkel.com

Edited by Ray Vallese
rjvallese@gmail.com. You can also find him on Facebook, Google+, and Twitter.

Published by 3lb Games LLC
www.3lbgames.com
ISBN 978-0-9848929-2-1

Limited edition, 1st printing: December 2011

DEDICATION

This book is dedicated to the three most important women in my life: my daughter, my wife, and my mother, and to the two most important men: my son and my stepfather. To the family I grew with, and the family I'm growing. Your support and your love are my world, the walls of which can face the fiercest storms.

PROLOGUE

He rode, his proud face bleeding and grim in the light of the setting sun. He cradled a sleeping baby in the crook of his left arm, the reins of the metal horse in his right fist. With a few swift kicks, he urged the steed ever faster westward. His eyes squinted into the setting sun, and beads of perspiration—or were they tears?—coursed down his unlined cheeks. The gleaming hooves of the steed tore great clumps of sod from the grassy hills as it sped through the spring dusk.

Miles behind him, the city burned on its mountain. Steel-clad knights thundered from the great city's gates into the dying day on their own metal stallions or took to the air with mechanical wings. The military dirigibles *Retaliator* and *Heaven's Will* rose slowly from the heart of the city, flames spitting from their engines, and turned their massive noses to the west.

The knights sought the oathbreaker, the thief of their princess, the betrayer of their king. They swore bloody vengeance on Pelagir of the King's Chosen, son of Pelgram, and raced to be the first to have his head. He had betrayed the most sacred of their oaths, and their rage burned as brightly as the flames in the capital city.

Childhood's Tale

Spring, Clasping Year 577

Three . . . four . . . five . . .

Pelagir's hands wrapped tightly around the straps of the whipping post.

Six . . .

Hot dust in his nostrils.

Seven . . .

Wet warmth on his back.

Eight . . .

Underneath the pain of the whip, he whispered a mantra:

Nine . . .

(you are a knight's son a knight's son)

Ten . . .

(KNIGHT'S SON KNIGHT'S SON)

Eleven . . .

The pain vanished deep within him, each lash of the whip a silvery explosion fading into the darkness.

Twelve . . .

His mind was blank for the final stroke. He might as well have been dead for all the pain it caused him.

It was his twelfth birthday. This punishment was nearly routine by now. Punishment for insubordination, for failing to complete his chores, for anything that angered his father... and Sir Pelgram had a notoriously short temper, especially since Pelagir's mother had left his cruel hand six years prior; Pelgram said she had fled home, but neighbors whispered of darker things. Pelagir hardly remembered her: the black hair, a tearful face, and the smell of flour with her embraces. But she had fled, and for all Pelagir knew, she could be dead now. He loathed her for her disappearance even as he secretly enshrined the ideal of her memory into his heart. He came into no contact with women, unless it was while collecting food from the market, and his interactions were no more than necessary to complete his transactions.

The casual slaps, disdain, and occasional beatings that once were her burden became her son's, and they increased in frequency and severity. Whippings could be had any time. Today it was for some imagined impudence, and Pelagir knew better than to protest his punishment.

His father was one of the Knights Faithful and burned to be more, but his desire was too strong and his flesh too weak. He spent his rage on the enemies of the Empire, and when none were available, he spent it on his son Pelagir. He said that he wanted to make his son one of the finest of the knights, and Pelgram knew that the Knights Elite had their feelings beaten out of them. Well, as he had said more than once, he'd bring his boy to them ready, and through his son his own glory would grow.

Pelgram's cruel nature was mirrored in his lean face. His black hair was shot through with streaks of iron gray, and his mustache was beginning to turn as well. His lean body was covered in scars from countless battles, and when he wore no shirt, Pelagir used to try to count them.

Pelagir's face was that of his father, and he was already almost as tall as his sire. He was not extraordinarily strong yet, despite the endless exercises his father forced upon him, but his relentless endurance made him the equal of any boy on the field.

Pelagir used to live for the times when his father was away on campaign. But now that he was twelve, he would be expected to travel with his father as a squire. He had only two options: continue to suffer the lash, or flee.

He chose to suffer. He chose the long path that could lead him to the place his father had failed to reach. He taught himself silence at the whipping post, taught himself to overcome pain, and buried the small voice within him that cried out at the injustice his father doled out.

His face betrayed none of this as he let go of the post and picked up his shirt, slipping it over the burning welts on his back without a grimace. His father had already turned away, telling him that dinner had best be ready by the time Pelgram returned from the knights' headquarters.

Pelagir watched his father stride away, and though his face did not show it, he prayed for his father's death.

Summer, CY 577

In Glendavy, the rebellious northeastern province of the Empire, Pelagir stood watch over his father, a bloody sword in his hand. Shouts rang out across the battlefield, the din of sword striking metal or flesh, the firing of the heavy artillery behind. Muffled explosions and screams. And Pelagir, unshaking, his cold eyes on a Glendavin man moving toward the unconscious knight and the boy guarding the fallen body. The man didn't seem to notice the body of his compatriot at the boy's feet as well.

The Glendavin grinned through his bushy red beard, hefting his axe as he hiked the short rise, and he began to chuckle as he drew near.

"Boy, step away from that knight and you'll live to see another battlefield. I'll just be having that armor, and we'll let the crows have the rest."

"You will not have it."

"I'm giving you a chance to live, lad. Best take it while you can."

"Your friend here thought the same thing."

The Glendavin's eyes widened for a moment. "You killed him?"

"Yes."

"How old are you, boy?"

"Twelve."

The man whistled. "That's impressive work. I killed my first at fifteen. Lost count since then." He chuckled, but Pelagir kept silent. "Not much for praise, are you, boy?"

"No." Pelagir's whippings had taught him to keep his face tight, and though he did not show it, terror was twisting his bowels.

"Nor do you talk much."

"No." Pelagir shifted his stance slightly, trying to remember the training his father had beaten into him.

"Then let me do the talking. How about you step aside and let me at that armor, and I'll take you back to Glendavy? We could use fighters, and it's better you come away now. Look." He held his bloody axe held loosely in his hand, confident in his ability, and gestured across the battlefield with his left. "The Empire's lost this battle already, and the scavengers will be coming out soon enough. It all looks like it's still in flux, but the fact is, it's over and your side—"

Pelagir executed a perfect lunge, his sword piercing the man's throat and emerging from the back of the neck. The man fell to his knees, his axe only halfway raised, struggling to strike back. But the axe fell from his fingers, and he touched the blade of the sword as if to pull it from his neck. He gasped three times, vomited blood, and Pelagir withdrew the blade with a clean stroke.

Pelgram moaned, and Pelagir knelt at his side, eager to take the praise his father would surely give. *Maybe,* Pelagir thought, *maybe this will mean I've proven myself at last.*

"What's happened?" Pelgram's eyes fluttered, came into focus.

"You were knocked unconscious by that man, there. I killed him. The other man came for your armor. I killed them both."

"Where's my mount?" Pelgram struggled to his knees, bracing himself on his son's shoulder, panting, shaking while his head settled.

"It was destroyed. That's why I had to defend you."

"From two whole Glendavins?" Scorn filled Pelgram's voice. "Find me a mount, and give me that sword." He pushed himself up, hard, and nearly forced Pelagir into the mud. For a moment, Pelagir imagined his honorable father falling to the ground with his son's twice-bloodied blade buried in his gut, Pelagir laughing as his father's blood spilled on his hands. But instead, the boy passed the hilt to his father and descended the rise to seek a mount for his father, the knight.

Fall, CY 577

Pelagir stood outside his father's library, his back straight, listening to the murmuring from inside the room. The messenger had ridden down from the hilltop, and Pelagir had barely had time to announce the visitor to his father when the man swept in behind him and closed the lad out of the library. Pelagir waited outside the door in case he was needed.

Behind the thick door, he could hear their muffled voices. The visitor's voice was calm and measured, his father's tense and clipped. Pelagir strained to hear the words, but could not. He knew that if he placed his ear to the door, all would become clear, but he had been caught at that once before, and he was not the sort of boy who made the same mistake twice. He waited, his body still and patient, but his mind raced as he explored the possibilities.

The man was clearly of some importance and, based on his bearing, was likely a knight. The messenger outranked his father or represented someone who did, or else (if Pelgram's voice was any indicator) he would have been shown the door minutes ago. Neither had asked for refreshment, so this was not a courtesy call. Orders, perhaps? Was his father being given command, or was he being commanded? More likely the latter, decided Pelagir, and they were commands Pelgram did not like.

In a short while, his father opened the door. "In, boy." Pelagir stepped inside. The rider stood in front of the desk, facing the door, his hands clasped behind him. He was not a tall man, but he was imposing regardless in his quiet strength. He waited to speak until Pelgram had closed the door and taken a position behind Pelagir.

"I am Lieutenant Caltash. I come from the knighthood." Pelagir straightened instantly. "I have spoken with your father already, and though he disagrees with your readiness, I have overridden his objections. In three weeks, you are to report to the academy for our advanced training. Congratulations, Pelagir. I'll be keeping my eye on you." With a meaningful glance at Pelgram, Caltash strode from the room. Pelgram followed on his footsteps to see his guest from the house, and Pelagir considered his future.

Knighthood was not a guarantee. Many of those who entered the academy failed. Some died. Some amounted to little more than squires or support—valuable in times of war and peace, no doubt, but what boy dreams of reaching glory through the quartermaster's ranks? What would he do if he washed out? Return home? No, he decided, he would sooner flee the capital Terona, perhaps to the duchies to work for one of the High Houses, or even to the provinces.

When Pelgram returned, his eyes had filled with a dark fury. He clenched his fists at his side, rather than strike his son, and said, "They say you're in shape. You're not. Your chores will double, your exercises will take an additional two hours, and we'll be carefully reviewing your lessons. I will not be shamed by your ineptitude in the eyes of the knighthood. If we're lucky, you won't be drummed out in the first year. If we're exceptionally lucky, you may even be accepted into the order of Knights Faithful, but I don't expect that."

He pointed toward the door. "Go. Your play time has ended. It's time for you to act like a man now and do a man's work."

Pelgram never laid the whip on his son again, though he clearly wished it when Pelagir stumbled under the weight of exhaustion. Pelagir thought his father's obsession with his son's imagined bad behavior (or as his father put it, "my dishonor") crumpled under the fear of the thought of what the Council of Knights would do to him if he sent them a recruit with fresh stripes across his back. The older man contented himself with curses, threats, and humiliations.

This was how Pelagir ended his childhood and took the first steps that led him toward manhood. Surely, he thought, surely the knighthood could be no worse.

THE GENERAL'S TALE

I write this letter now to send to you, children of my friends, in hopes that I will be able to deliver it to you by pigeon or by hand. Perhaps they will have told you of my rise; I know that I have played the part of uncle to you, and have not spoken of my past. Perhaps you know this history already. If so, I ask your forgiveness. If not, I hope to educate you.

I write this morning from a small inn in one of the lower quarters of the city. I can hear the bells in the High Cathedral toll eight of the clock. I believe that this is the last chance I will have to write these notes, and I beg you to forgive their lack of flower. The words I put to paper here are based on my recollection, not set down with perfect accuracy. I am no scribe, and I may have missed words, intonations, or phrases that might have changed the meaning of the events I describe here. Forgive me my errors.

Forces have been set in motion, forces I can only struggle against. I cannot hope to control them, and I believe that they are already poised to sweep me under, to dash me against the rocks in the current they have created.

I cannot send a note to warn the king of my suspicions. After the conversation I had in the garden this morning, I think the conspirators watch and perhaps control any messages the king receives. I must find a way to put this message into the world, and perhaps a solution will come to me before I have finished writing. Still, I have written to three of my lieutenants: Ilocehr Hargrave, William "Wet" M'Cray, and Nansa Westkitt. I trust them implicitly and with my life, and with their help perhaps we can find a way together to work against the Empire's enemies.

My window is open. The candles flicker in the slight breeze, which carries the scent of the ivy and flowers outside. I can hear thunder rumble distantly. It's getting louder. The storm tonight will be a bad one, I think... but I digress. It is time to begin.

My full name is Tomas Glasyin. I am of the Lesser House Stoyan. Our matriarch swears fealty to House Westkitt, yet when I took my oath in the army, I became Houseless. I am a general in the Empire's armies, and until recently, I was a high commander of the ground forces. Tomorrow, I might be dead.

They say that victory is sweet. I have never found it so. Though it is better than the alternative, far better, victory tastes like ashes to me.

I remember the last time I killed someone with my own hands. It was fifteen years ago, during the Utland Uprising, and the enemy had broken through our lines. I was confident of victory, but not so sure that I would live to see it. I had planned for the line breaking as a ruse, to draw in our foes to be crushed by our reserves, but the enemy fought with greater ferocity than I would have credited and turned the break closer than I anticipated. A fair number of my staff had let their combat skills slip, and because of that, I found myself face to face with an enemy for the first time in years.

My talents were true, and my muscles remembered their training. I bested the three who came against me before my troops rallied around me. I led the counter-charge myself when I discovered that Colonel William M'Cray, leader of the left flank, had been slain with his commanders. I held the flank until I could withdraw to oversee the greater battle. I dispatched perhaps five more of the enemy before the reserve pounded in and I could return to the command quarters. I remember the faces of each of the dead men. It is a facility I have, to remember names and faces, and I can summon up the dying agonies of the hundreds I have killed in my life.

As I said, I killed only eight that night, a far cry from the battles of my youth. I do not wish to take credit for the actions of my men, who fought bravely and well. I will claim credit for my quick action and for keeping morale, and because of that, I can claim credit for victory that day. That triumph led to the suppression of the Utland Uprising, and so I can call it the turning point in that conflict. For that, I can claim credit for holding the Empire together, since the other rebellious counties and provinces saw that we meant to hold our land no matter the cost, and their mutterings subsided. The king saw this as well, and he awarded me the Star of Ydris, an honor given to soldiers of exceptional bravery and valor.

There have been only twenty-five stars awarded in the fifteen-hundred year history of the Empire, only twelve in the nearly six hundred Clasping Years since Terona's last great acquisition, and I hold two of them.

I say all this to establish my credentials, not to boast. Despite my accomplishments, I take no joy in victory. I look on the fields of the dead and I cringe. I order the devastation of cities and towns and I weep inside at the destruction. Time and trouble have taught me to avoid war at all costs. As a younger man, I desired glory on the battlefield, but no longer. It is a last resort, and I curse the necessity of my profession. I have never told this to anyone. I am a private man, and I keep my agonies to myself. If it were not for my leadership, the senior general would be someone more reckless, less skillful, and the cost of war would be more than I could bear. I do the job I hate because there is no one who can do it better—no one who could do it at even twice the cost in lives. That is no choice at all. I serve the Empire and the king that I love.

I have led men in the Imperial armies for thirty-nine years in one capacity or another. I did not rise up through the ranks. I was born into a powerful family and was placed well when it became apparent that I had an aptitude for leadership. It is a common misconception among the troops that if they work hard enough, they can achieve the rank I hold. This is untrue. The command of the armies is a privilege the rich and the wealthy guard jealously, no matter the qualifications of those below them, and there are still many appointments to the higher ranks made purely the basis of blood. I admit that a number of these noble appointments are gifted, such as House Cronen's Count-General Beremany—but I will speak more of him later.

I will say that under my command, the upper echelons of the Imperial armies have become far more open to skillful men and women who suffered the accident of low birth, and someday there may yet be a commoner in my position. Not in the waning years of this century, though possibly in the next, if the Empire lasts that long. My aides and those around me are all of noble birth, but of the rank below that holds commoners in its arms, and they serve ably.

I pass word of their accomplishments upward when I can. I can only hope that the king will continue to listen to these praises, should he survive what I have recently discovered.

I understand that I am well loved by those under my command, at least as loved as a general can be. Though I am stern, and though I enforce a severe discipline among my troops, I am fair, and I see to it that those deserving reward are rewarded. I ride among them when I am able, so that they can see I do not despise their sacrifice, though I do not always share their worship— many of my troops are religious, but I have treated with the High Exegetes and the ecclesiastical courts, and they are rotten. While the teachings may be sound, the messengers are not—but I take care to conceal my feelings.

Morale among my people, male and female alike, is generally good, and I work hard to ensure that it remains as high as possible. I do not take luxuries when my troops suffer hardships. I go without when they must. I will not have them think that they must suffer so that I may live in leisure. They already see that when they look at the courtiers of the king. I have little use for courtiers—they do little honest work in their lives, instead preferring to aggrandize themselves through the sweat of others.

I toil in the courts of the king when I must, and I do mean toil—I would rather be among the troops, drilling and training and sweating, than passing among the courtiers who are eager to be seen reflected in my sometimes-meager glory. The camps are honest.

Though politics play a part in the decisions we make in the high councils of the army, I have done my best to make their resolutions as visible as possible, so that those under my command will know the reasons behind the orders that affect them. This does not make me popular with some of my more ambitious subordinates, and I have earned enemies in the king's court for my plain speaking, but I am close—or was close, at least—in the councils of the king. None at court dared curry my disfavor. They know my disdain for Imperial adventure, and there have been times when my words have turned back declarations of war, especially war that would serve only to benefit interests of certain nobles in the court. I dislike politics because I am at a decided disadvantage among the courtiers who practice that skill even in their sleep. Still, I have served my king with integrity and loyalty since the time he rode to campaign with us as a prince.

I value my men, and I love the Empire, though it has fallen into decay. I try to hold back the decay as long as I can. I do not know if even I can do this. It might be too late. No, I am certain it is. My time has passed.

It is now ten of the clock.

I first distinguished myself around forty years ago, when I was but eighteen. My father had just secured me a place on the general staff of the Third Army. I served as a page to General Jon Hawkins, the infamous Butcher of Greenfield. Mine was an honorable job, I suppose, but it was designed to keep me clear of combat, out of harm's way, and to show how useful I could be to those in power.

My father clearly wanted me to stand out from the others, and he raised me as only a baron's son can be raised. I received instruction in dancing, etiquette, and some of the other arts, but I excelled only in strategy and weapons craft. I would have made an imperfect courtier, but as my father had no other vision for my future, I had no choice but to continue with the course he assigned. I suppose I should thank him for his interest in my future, but he is long dead, felled by an assassin's blade at the height of the troubles thirty-five years ago, in the Birdsnest Wars sparked by the death of the old king. My father was a bit player in that drama between the powerful Houses, but he aligned himself stupidly when he could have stepped aside with honor. He could have bettered himself by remaining neutral in a clash of giants—neutrality would have put him in good stead no matter who won. Instead, he made just enough partisan fuss that his sentence was sealed. I was lucky they did not kill me as well. I have never investigated his death, though I have a good idea who ordered it. She is dead now, and naming names would serve only to inflame passions better left to heal. And if I were mistaken, why, that would be worse.

My father's death showed me that politics is a more dangerous battleground than the fields of war—certainly a good deal more treacherous.

By the time of his murder, however, I had ensconced myself firmly in the military, nearly beyond the reach of his particular enemies, and too valuable to the Empire to be punished for his sins.

I digress again.

General Hawkins was brilliant, with a knowledge of strategy and tactics so deep it was practically instinctive. When I was permitted to remain in his tent for any length of time, I learned more than I ever had learned in the training schools, and the more level-headed tactics of Hawkins have led me through many a battle safely and well. He earned his nickname, though, for he did not care if he brought suffering and destruction as long as he achieved his goal, and he loved nothing more than to lead his troops personally so that he might taste the blood of his foes. There were many in his staff who felt as he did, declaring that diplomacy and respect are the battleground of the courtier, that we in the armies were simply the muscle behind the words and should commit ourselves fully to the craft of death. That attitude led us nearly to the brink of destruction.

I entered the army and the general staff during a time of peace, during the old king's final attempts at negotiations with the Siullans to the east. As the history books tell us, those attempts were doomed to failure, and they failed not long after they began, a year into my service. The people of both sides wanted peace, but our rulers had no heart for it. Outwardly, they called for calm, but between themselves, they understood that the negotiations would ultimately bear no fruit. Furthermore, the Siullan leaders understood that old King Fannon III offered them nothing but a golden servitude. They had their pride. They answered him.

The Siullans laid explosives throughout the city of Amchester that fall. Ten thousand died, among them the ambassador to the Siullans. Their senators denied responsibility, but both they and we knew it was their answer to our proposition. King Fannon called upon General Hawkins to speak to their answer.

The general mustered two of the Empire's seven armies, and led the First and Third east in the heavy autumn rains, creating two massive, curved pincer arms that measured over fifty miles long from end to end. (The Second and the Fourth were both armies whose ranks brimmed with soldiers from our eastern provinces, and we did not want their loyalty tested—we always send warriors who have little connection to the land they'll conquer so that they do not falter at the sight of a friend's face.) The First Army was to the north, the Third to the south. We had nearly one hundred thousand men in the field. The Siullans had perhaps sixty thousand. We had six military dirigibles, twenty scouting dirigibles, artillery, and the knights—both Elite and the lesser orders—and our troops were simply better trained. It would be, in truth, no contest. We couldn't understand why the Siullans didn't surrender and save themselves.

We should have put ourselves in their place. The destruction that happened later was a failure of our empathy and a failure of our intelligence.

Our scouts ranged out ahead of us as we crossed the hilly border into Siull. They rode the silver steeds of the Knights Elite, the metal-armored, unliving creatures created by the Archmagus and his apprentices. These were smaller, slimmer mounts, faster than the coursers of the knights, but not nearly as durable; I have seen them explode in gouts of flame and flying shrapnel from a single well-placed arrow. Still, they traveled far faster than any ordinary horse, such as the rest of us were compelled to ride, and a smart scout would rather throw a leg in front of an arrow than let it strike her mount—if she were foolish enough to travel within bowshot in the first place. The scouting steeds were nearly as valuable as the scouting dirigibles we had above us, and certainly stealthier. We did not have the flight troops we have now, those unsavory creatures of the magi.

The Siullans gave way steadily before us, and our lines extended as we struggled to encircle them. They burned the farms and villages behind them as they went, of course, to keep us from their bounty, and because they knew the Siullan Republic was doomed. They wished us to have no profit from their death. We'd have done the same thing.

The scouts reported that the Siullan numbers dwindled daily. Some of the Siullans rode ahead of their main army, and the tiny bands disappeared in the hills through which we marched. Sometimes, scouts who sought these bands disappeared. Hawkins was not especially suspicious, for many of these deserters had reemerged as guerrillas to harass our lines, and we found enough of our dead scouts near the shattered, smoking remains of their coursers. We lost two scouting dirigibles, brought down by lucky shots from their rolling without injudiciously exposing their rear flank. They were trapped, exactly where Hawkins wanted them.

Students of military history will know that we were exactly where they wanted us.

I will not recount here the full particulars of what happened next. Let us say that the Siullans had lured us into precisely the kind of ambush to which our massive armies were so vulnerable. They had laced the ground in the hills surrounding the Gaurin Plains with a network of caverns and tunnels over the years in preparation for an eventuality such as this. Explosive charges awaited detonation under our feet, with iron bulwarks between blast areas to protect the men and women lurking in wait for the signal to attack from below. It was deadly in its ingenuity and astonishing in its foresight.

The Siullans struck at night. I suspect their first move was to send an assassin to climb the lines into one of our heavy dirigibles. The sudden fiery crash of the airship into the heart of our army was the signal for the detonation of the explosives in the caves, and that detonation was the signal for the ten thousand in the caves to rise up and murder us in the tents where we plotted the next day's action. Our guards were wary, but many of them were taken completely by surprise. The screaming slaughter was the final signal for their army to rush the lines of the Third Army. It seemed they had no intention of survival. They wanted us to suffer as much as possible before their republic went the way of all who opposed our Empire.

The dirigible crash was frighteningly close to Hawkins's tent, close enough that the great flaming struts of the flying machine set the tents afire with their shrapnel, close enough that the shock waves knocked the supports out from under the pavilions. Those inside the tents of the staff were trapped under the material, and many of them roasted or suffocated in the choking smoke within the canvas folds. I had had enough presence of mind to equip myself with a wrist knife, which I carried and still carry at all times, and it saved my life.

14

When I had cut a hole through the canvas, I looked upon a scene from the first of Hell's blasted plains. Twisted, blackened struts skewed at crazy angles. A rolling, roaring landscape of fire and smoke lit the air from all sides, and shadows cast from the flames cut like knives through the soot and ash that billowed from the ground. Screams rose from the tents all around me as the canvas took fire and turned the tents' interiors into ovens, waxy fat running liquid from the seams of the blazes. Figures silhouetted against the light raised dripping swords and plunged them into their victims with unimaginable ferocity, howling their vengeance upon us.

I dug my sword from the smoldering canvas and sought to save the people I could save. Those in the midst of flames were clearly too far gone. I sought first those who were still struggling in the fallen tents that were near combustion, and those whose tents were flickering with the beginnings of inferno. Around me, other quick-thinking soldiers did the same. I must have saved a good twenty of the staff, junior officers and attachÈs, before I came on Hawkins's tent. I suppose if I had been more ambitious, I would have run there first, but I cut the doomed free as I went instead—a bad strategy on my part, but one for which I cannot blame myself.

Hawkins's tent was aflame, and there was but one figure in it who still struggled, faintly. The stench of seared human flesh had filled my nose for several minutes, so I was spared the smell of those roasting inside. I slashed the canvas, and black smoke billowed out into my face. I thrust my arm into the rent, seized the trapped man inside, pulled him to safety, and came face to face with General Hawkins. He was badly burnt, his face seared and blistered. He was missing his eyebrows and a fair-sized patch of hair, and he vomited on me as the fresh air hit his lungs. Two raiders came our way then, and as the general struggled to breathe, I beat their weapons aside and skewered them.

When Hawkins pulled himself together—surprisingly quickly—he armed himself with a raider's sword and began to bark commands to the surviving officers of his staff. Inside a few moments, we had the beginning of an actual resistance to the attack.

We had a functioning command structure from top down within half an hour of the disaster, despite being hit in our most vulnerable spot; it was a mark of the discipline Hawkins had drilled into his troops. Ten minutes after the commands flew again, we had resistance to the Siullan guerillas. The ten thousand enemies in our camp tried to prevent us from organizing a response to the forty thousand Siullans rushing our lines, but failed. Our training was too complete to allow us to fall into disarray. The outlying troops were, in the main, unaffected by the explosions, but they had to deal immediately with the full force of the Siullans and could not return to aid the rest of the army. Neither could they expect reinforcements or leadership from us, and they were being slaughtered even as we got ourselves back on our feet.

Our remaining dirigibles fired explosives and shot glass vials of poisonous gas into the Siullan encampment, annihilating any who had not rushed the front lines, eliminating their artillery positions in choking, coughing death. We lost three of our strong dirigibles before their guns were made useless.

Nearly two thousand of our men had perished immediately in the explosions and campsite slaughter, and several thousand more fell before they rallied against the Siullan army. As our foes hadn't had the shock of seeing their command post obliterated in a cloud of flame and dust, they pressed us mercilessly, determined to inflict as much damage as possible before our other army wiped them out. Even with our swift response, it seems that we would have been defeated had it not been for the incredible speed of the Knights Elite of the First Army racing to our assistance. The infantry and cavalry followed as close behind as possible.

When the 4,000 knights (a mixture of Elite, Faithful, and Lesser) hit the Siullans from the rear, we thought at first that the sky had opened and delivered the angels of Kattriya to save us. Our knights laid into the Siullans with a bloody will, avenging our losses and pain with a fanatic fervor. Although their defeat was inevitable, the Siullans fought to their last breath, determined not to surrender to our dubious mercies. Of course, we were in no mood to show mercy. We slaughtered them wherever we found them. It was a grim night's work.

By morning, we had established hospitals for the soldiers wounded in the terror attack, and the knights had volunteered for the dangerous work of clearing the tunnels. Bloodlust was in their eyes, and Hawkins was wise enough to allow them free rein in exorcising it. The Knights Elite of the Third had taken heavy losses in the attack, more so than any other unit; they had set up their command camp directly over a lode of underground explosives, and the limbs of a good portion of them were strewn over the landscape when the attack began. The knights were also the quickest to recover, and if it were not for the fast thinking of their commander, I'd have had to face down a good number more of the Siullans at Hawkins's tent. The outcome of the battle might have been decidedly different.

I thought that my performance the night of the battle had gone unnoticed, but I should have known better. Hawkins called me into his tent, and he personally promoted me, giving me a squadron of my own troops to command with the promise that he'd keep an eye on me. He guaranteed me a medal when we returned to Terona. I had left the capital as a messenger. I returned a hero. My father was disappointed, though he struggled to hide it, and I knew that I had left the path he had chosen for me.

It is two in the afternoon already, and I cannot believe that I have had this long to write. You might ask why, if my time is limited, have I spent so much of my time writing about the past? It is a good question, and a fair one. My answer is this: we see the events of today being written in the pages of history. Small incidents unfold onto a massive scale. Loyalty in the past becomes the mechanism of betrayal.

The knights saved us then. They could save us now, if they only knew where to strike, and if I trusted their captain enough to tell him of the plot against the king. But the engineer of this rot in Terona plays a subtle game, and deep. The knights see the hand of someone in the diplomatic service, which of course is the polite name for our spies. Yet their commander realizes that if he sees a spy's work, surely it cannot be a spy—at least, not one of the spies we have trained, for ours are also subtle and deep. The captain has called for the executions of certain high-placed suspects. The king is not yet so addled that he'll agree to this, and I don't think the captain expects it to happen. I'm sure he and his second have assassins who are ready to strike at a word but have no idea where. Like all under his command, if he is not involved, I'm sure the captain longs for direct action and chafes when he is denied. The knights are full of powerful emotion, though they deny it to themselves, and that hidden passion drives them to excellence and fierce duty.

I share their frustration. I believe it may be one of the few emotions we do share. The knights are either more than human, or less. They lack something that drives the rest of us. Perhaps it is beaten out of them in their merciless training. Perhaps it is inculcated in them in place of honest human feeling. I know that I have seen innocent boys turned into blank-faced but burning killers, trained to become masters of any weapon I might care to name—though they prefer the humming weapons made by the Archmagus for each individual on the occasion of his knighting, and I do not blame them, for those magical blades are the finest I have seen men or women carry.

I am constantly amazed that mere humans would dare stand against the knights and their weapons. The knightly initiation, under the aegis of the Archmagus and his apprentices, trades a portion of their humanity for the blessings of strength and speed. After their three-day initiation, they emerge from their cloister wrapped in bloodstained bandages, and they have become inhuman. Though their training takes them far down the roads of experience all men know, it is the secret of their initiation that puts them beyond the boundaries of ordinary human knowledge.

It is this flaw that keeps them from the command of our armies. They are weapons themselves, and one does not trust a weapon to wage war, for it is a weapon's nature to seek blood and give no quarter. They are under the direct command of the king, whom they are trained to adore, whose life they guard with their own, the living embodiment of the Empire they serve. When on campaign, they are under the direct command of the senior general and exist side by side with the ordinary chain of rule, but they are strong-minded individuals, and if they were not so valuable in combat, they would have been disestablished long ago. In fact, they report mainly to their direct leaders, the commander and his captains, taking no order from any but him or me. They act as cavalry, as scouts, as infantry—in any warlike function possible. It takes a strong general to keep them in line, for they are willful and cruel.

It is good, then, that many of our generals are willful and cruel as well. They have to be, in order to prosecute the endless minor wars of the Empire. The Empire looks always outward, and it does so not only for its own glory but also to keep itself from looking inward. Should the populace turn away from its external enemies long enough to watch its own functioning, it is my belief that we would be torn apart from the rebellion that would surely follow in the next decade. I believe that it is my duty to press slowly on our enemies, though it benefits our nobles to move more quickly on their pet villains.

This is, of course, only my view, but it seems to fit. Why else would we not press aggressively on every tyrant we vilify? Why else would we allow them to grow in power? Our spies are skilled enough and our intelligence network swift enough that we can identify potential threats. The other nations of the world could, I suppose, unite against us at once, but even now I question whether they could overcome us. Possibly they could. Possibly their scattered magi have developed some sort of secret weapon. They could inflict grievous damage on us, but in return, they would suffer losses their lands could not sustain. In short, if we die, they die as well. That, at least, is how it falls out in my mind. It would take our beloved Empire to turn in upon itself for them to stand a chance of succeeding.

The signs are everywhere that this is about to happen.

The time is six in the evening. Night draws near. The storm is breaking out over the city, and the wind has a hold of my curtains.

Thirty-five years ago, I was in a good position to advance myself in the army. Because of my deeds in the Siullan affair, I had risen swiftly and fraternized with the sons of other nobles, including some of those in the High Houses. I do not know if you have kept current with the political maneuverings of the High Houses, though as children of the Lesser Houses it behooves you to understand them so that you can anticipate their moves and be prepared when they call upon your services.

The Empire balances their influences against each other, but each has its particular whims, goals, and strengths. All of them, of course, help to fund the military, help to patrol the borders, and pay to maintain the infrastructure that supports their takings. They maintain their private armies, with soldiers picked from our academies, but when their soldiers must muster under my command, they cast off their allegiances and their commanders to become soldiers of the Empire.

As the great families of the Empire, the descendants of King Martyn's supporters, they guard their prerogatives fiercely. They intermingle with one another, marrying each other for political gain, casting each other aside, and using the peasants to fight their battles with each other. Riots in the cities, food shortages, plagues—I have seen the High Houses use all of these to drive home a point to their momentary rivals, and sometimes even to their allies. By sowing unrest with their foes, they show their own control. The Empire holds these fractious and arrogant Houses at arm's length but doesn't dare to let them go any farther than that. They do not care about the populace except as a means to count the score against each other.

And now that I am no longer to be part of their society, I may say this openly: they parade their honor, but their influence runs deep beneath respectable society. I do not say that they are responsible for the criminal underworld, but they absolutely profit from it.

For instance, the Westkitt, those noted humanitarians and most charitable of the Houses, the strongest pillar of Father Church, carry on a brisk slave trade, sometimes even with our most vicious enemies, the Sjuri. Perhaps they are trying to buy their absolution with their tithes. Or take the Cronen: they provide most of the diplomats and ambassadors to our neutral neighbors and our enemies, but they also train assassins and malcontents to keep their enemies off-balance. They sell our secrets when the price is right. The House of Bhumar, one of the great shipping concerns and trade houses, does a brisk business in narcotics and other contraband. The Vukovi, our king's House, send traveling justices across the Empire to serve in places where knowledge of the law is sparse, preaching respect before the throne, and they simultaneously collect a portion of every bought ruling that their lackeys provide the wealthy. And let us not forget our mercantile masters, the House of Deng, whose largesse helps support the Imperial Bank, and who suck dry the lesser craftsmen and merchants.

The Lesser Houses like ours are still nobility to one degree or another, but our collective pedigree is not nearly as impressive. Perhaps these Houses were late converts to the growing empire, like the Micolli. They might have fallen from grace through the years, like the Torvalds who lost the East for a century. They simply lack the requisite ferocity to prove themselves and thus watch their holdings seep away to their competitors—like the House of Glasyin, regrettably, who became vassals to the Stoyan. They might have been rewarded for later services, as were the Huldens, who helped the Deng establish the banking system in these last three hundred years.

We might still provide certain services to the Church or the Council of Magi, and our children fill the ranks of the knighthood, but we simply cannot break the stranglehold the High Houses have on the court. I do not say this to belittle you or your potential accomplishments, but to tell you what the situation looks like from Terona. We must realize that the High Houses see us as pawns in their games, useful tools or fading glories but ultimately no more than occasional breeding stock when they don't need to secure alliances with their competitors.

Most of the nobles with whom I met were useless militarily and served mainly as a way to distinguish themselves before they moved on to fill the court with their plots and gossip. I dismissed them as foppish dandies then, though I realized the necessity of keeping them, if not friendly, at least tolerant toward me and my designs.

I am, in hindsight, aware of the irony of judging them for their plots while I engaged in mine. In my defense, allow me to argue that I worked for the good of the country as I saw it, struggling to prevent its inevitable downfall, to slow the slide into anarchy. Their plots were for personal aggrandizement. Mine was to serve something that was worthy of my service. That is what I told myself then. Perhaps the lies we tell ourselves become truer the more strongly we believe them.

I had just begun to earn the friendship of Prince Fannon, nephew of the king, when word came that Fannon III had passed, succumbing at last to the inevitable stroke of age. Though it was expected that he would die, no one was prepared for it so soon. No sooner had we heard of his death than the hyenas were upon the corpse and ambition began to tear the army apart. The death of the king brought us to the Birdsnest Wars, in which the High Houses sought to position themselves to take advantage of the chaos. They took themselves to the Birdsnest, King Martyn's old summer mansion on the hills outside of Terona, and pressed their claims to the throne, describing the deeds they had done for the Empire and the blessings they had secured for the many. They outlined their lineage, and described why their lines were closer to the bloodline of Martyn. They presented their presumptive heirs. The highest officers of the forces turned away from their sworn service to defend the country and brought their strength to bear for their chosen House. Whole divisions went to fight for the Westkitts and the Dengs and the Bhumari, and companies and battalions split for the Lesser Houses.

A few remained standing with Prince Fannon. Fannon III had died childless, and though his decree should have rendered his nephew the legitimate heir, questions of legality and the prince's legitimacy made what should have been an orderly succession a time of blood. I supported the prince, as did a number of the nobles who were unconvinced that their Houses deserved the throne. We had the Vukovi, whose judges and heralds outlined Fannon's right, but who listens to the niceties of the law when such power is at stake? We believed that Fannon had shown the qualities necessary to lead us, and this was more than belief in his lineage. Men and women alike believed that the Empire deserved existence more than their own House did, and though I suspected at least three of our compatriots of passing information to their superiors, my suspicions were entirely unfounded. I was grateful to be proven wrong.

"I will see you all rewarded," Prince Fannon told us. We believed in his confidence, and we believed in his right to rule.

"Seek others loyal to me," he said. "Turn them against their brethren if you must. Remind them of their duty." And so we did. We traveled among the House armies, speaking to the lesser officers, to the enlisted men, promising them riches, rank, forgiveness. Some came with us. Some denied us. Some sought to betray us, and these we slew. Slowly our numbers swelled, even as the High Houses tore one another apart with their vicious battles and assassins and poisons.

The prince, for his part, went to the Knights Elite. They remained above it, guarding the Imperial Palace, watching, impassive. When the prince, muffled and disguised, managed at last to win through to their commander, his answer was brief: "Show us that you can command men, and we shall be yours to command."

"Watch me," Prince Fannon said, "and you shall see."

When the prince returned to us, his inexperienced general staff, his command to us was to pick a battle that we might win. Our numbers were less than half those of any of the Lesser Houses—as far as we could tell, none of the High Houses even knew we existed. I realize now that of course they did; their spy networks covered and still cover the spheres of influence that the Houses think matter. They were watching us as a matter of keeping their eyes on the prince during this rite of fire. I just don't think they believed he could manage it. After all, who did he have on his side? A handful of officers, each with a small troop of men, some minor House backing (purely as a political gambit), and the royal name. Fannon, who grew up in the intrigues of the Houses, knew their capabilities, and he guided our hands as we laid the groundwork for his assumption of the throne. We faced three assassins, and we were surprised we did not see more.

The apparatus of Empire turned ever onward as our drama played out.

Prince Fannon saw something in me. Perhaps it was the kinship born of arms. Whatever the reason, he and I plotted and planned his resumption of the throne most intently. We laid traps for the High Houses, building their suspicions and their enmities, setting snares for them from their old histories. We played on the insults and slights they had dealt one another for centuries, and through our few contacts in the court, we amplified their grievances. We fought them in the words of aristocrats, through propaganda, through small acts of generosity to the common man—and most of all, through their rivals.

The details are unimportant now, though our small victories were glorious. I still admire our scheme to turn the proud Cronens against the money-loving Dengs. With a little coin and the hint of more to come to the DeTrellzis (one of the Cronen's Lesser Houses), a few judiciously placed words to the knight-aspirants of their House, and some careful research into their past histories, we set off a feud between the two that lasted for a week and took the hottest of their heads to the grave. By the time it and half a dozen other feuds like it had ended, we had made our move for the throne.

These feuds were not without cost to us. My father, that ambitious and naive soul, tried to play peacemaker in the middle of one of them. His involvement was not our doing. I don't think he knew he was being played by one of our enemies. I am sure they told him the truth before they slit his throat and left his body in the street for the dogs. Though he and I had had our differences, I burned to take revenge. The prince had different ideas.

"Our plans are too close to fruition," he said, "and I need your attention here."

"But my father—"

"Your father was a pawn, in life and in death! They're using him to distract you when I need you most, and if you pursue your revenge now, then everything we have done here will be for nothing. I ask you to reconsider."

"The blood of my family has been spilled. I *will* have my revenge."

"Then you will choose between the command of my armies and your revenge. I will not order your obedience in this."

Thirty-five years have passed since then, and I still have not had revenge. By the time we had taken the throne and gained the obedience of the knights, our energies were expended on keeping the Empire together and building a coalition of the Houses against the rioting populace, who had seen the chaos and feared for the safety of the Empire. I could not set aside my duty, and still cannot. Even now, when I believe that my silence serves no purpose, I will not take the risk of tearing our fragile alliances apart and turning to mob rule.

It is now nine in the evening. The sun has left the sky, and the storm has opened over the city.

Swiftly, then, swiftly! I have little more time to dote on the past. In the many years I have had the honor and the privilege of serving under His Majesty Fannon IV, I have watched the fortunes of the Empire

24

increase. Yet even as the surface of the Imperial painting grew in luster, so did the canvas underneath it rot, falling apart under the pressing weight of time and the teeth of countless vermin, teeming with corruption and spite. The Empire is strong from without, but from within it awaits the slightest push to start it crumbling.

The signs were there. What began as a proud land so many hundreds of years ago, rising from the chaos of the Great Uprising on the back of King Martyn the Strong, has lost its way, become adrift in the endless plots of the minor lords and nobles who scheme in Terona. Each High House maneuvers against the others. Each pursues its own vendettas at the cost of the Empire, each with its own vision of Martyn's dream, each doing its level best to play kingmaker, and now I cannot think of anything that might hold them together. Except perhaps the traitors' plot—but I shudder to think of what they intend should they succeed.

How did I first become aware of the traitors? In the easiest way possible: they approached me. It wasn't anything as simple as asking me to betray His Majesty, but to my eye, it may as well have been.

It was a night about a week ago when they approached me. I was in the court, mingling among the courtiers with the three trusted lieutenants I mentioned previously: William "Wet" M'Cray of House Cronen, the son of the man who had died in the Utland Uprising, was the first. He was a tall, slim, and nervous man, but his mind was keen and fast, and with a rapier I knew none better among mortal men. The second was Ilocehr Hargrave, a captain lately of of House Bhumar, a dark-skinned man of wild impetuosity, generosity of spirit, and a fierce grasp of small squad tactics. He was also, it was rumored, seeking the hand of Sofia DeTrellzi, and this led to no end of hardship for him among his peers. The third was Nansa Westkitt, who had been third in line to inherit the power of the Westkitts when the matriarch passed away, but this peaceable young woman had discovered a talent for supply that outshone the appeals of Father Church, and she renounced her family's calling for ours. All of them noble-born, and all of them well equipped to help me find the mood among the powerful.

This was our most hated duty: courtier work, necessary to find out what they wanted from us. Would they be seeking to expand the frontier skirmishes, or were they content with the progress of our many tiny flares of fighting? Did they seek intensification or a withdrawal based on the success or failure of their business dealings? Would we be drawn into another Siullan conflict to fortify the coffers of the wealthy? My staff and I did not like to be caught unaware of such things, and the spy network I had built was not experienced enough to deal with the many wiles of the court. As I excused myself from the company of the Dowager Duchess of Garand, I found young Viscount DeBow at my elbow. He was a slim fellow, blond, short, favoring clothing of plain browns. He was also a member of the Vukovi, which, to my knowledge, required none of the military's services at this time.

"Your Excellency," he said, "may I have a moment of your time?"

"Of course, Viscount." I bowed. "How may I serve you?" He engaged me immediately in a conversation of little import, gossip and the like. I thought at first that he was attempting to gain a favor for a relative in the military, or that he had suggestions as to the deployment of troops in some skirmish or another. I paid him rote responses and took little heed of his prattle until he said, "General Glasyin, do you love the Empire?"

I gave him my full attention. A small smile danced behind his lips. I replied evenly, "I would give my life for it." He bowed and excused himself. As he left, I replayed the conversation quickly through my mind. Was he a spy from some cabal? Had my enemies on the council convinced Fannon that I required a loyalty check? Had I said or done anything that might throw my love of and duty to the land into doubt, even after all these years? What about my service to the king? I have been in the Imperial court for decades now, and this callow youth had just warned me I was being watched. But under whose direction? I could go to no one if I wanted to see how this played out. If I wished to expose potential corruption, I could not speak to the king's advisors, for that would reveal my loyalties immediately. I resolved to be more careful with my words in the future, that I might discover the truth. I said nothing to my men, which I bitterly regret now.

I did not have long to wait. Within a few days, at another gathering in the court in which the courtiers discussed the wildfire uprisings and the small peasant revolts, the Baroness of Imlay, a vassal of House Deng, caught me alone as I filled my drink. I thought she might wish to talk about this "self-rule" that some of the western teachers and ecclesiasts were preaching, but instead she engaged me in a meaningless conversation on military history, focusing mainly on our victories and the glories our armies and diplomats had won. As she spoke, I began to get the uncomfortable sense that while these might be her words, the sentiment in her speech had been planted in order to draw me out. When she began to contrast the Empire of old with the Empire of the modern day and spoke of decay and rebirth, I knew for certain.

"Baroness, do you suggest that our Empire has stagnated, that we are past the ability to reach for glory?"

"No, General, but I do suggest that, just as a man weakens if he does not constantly exercise himself, so too could the body politic lose strength if it remains inert. As this body loses strength, its enemies must see its enervation as opportunity."

"So instead of saying we are past the point of no return," I replied, "you suggest that we waste away through lack of ambition."

"I do," she said, "and in the end, apathy leads to death. We must surely do something. Would you not agree that weakness left untreated leads to death?"

"I cannot disagree."

"And therefore, as with the body, the Empire must again exercise itself if it is not to fall prey to debilitating illness?"

"I concede the point.

"Then all that is required of us is to begin the process of motion. And where else does this process begin in the body but in the brain?"

"And you suggest that we motivate the brain to begin the exercise anew?" I said. "Surely you understand that the king is not eager to embark on any new ventures, not with his new child consuming his attention, nor with the tax situation being what it is. Indeed, I see this time as one of great precariousness. It is our duty to tread carefully so as to prevent utter chaos."

"It is a time to walk carefully, or a time to act decisively. Glasyin, you have seen many of these moments in your life as a leader. You must know when it is time to act."

"I would first hear your proposal. Grand rhetoric is useful for stirring to action, but carefully planned deeds direct the unformed into a useful shape."

"What makes you think that I have a proposal?" she said.

"It would be a pity," I replied, "if this were simply idle talk. Indeed, if this *were* simply idle talk, it might be construed as treason."

She studied my face carefully. "Thank you for your words and your time, General. I hope to speak to you again soon."

"I hope to understand your position on the subject more deeply," I said, and sketched a bow. When I straightened, she had moved into the crowd in the shadows under the high, vaulted ceiling.

So. It was a plot, then, a plot aimed at the very heart of the Empire. And clearly they had the tacit support of at least two High Houses, or were making an effort to appear as if they did. By approaching me, they had as much as said that they thought my duty to the Empire was greater than my loyalty to the king—and they clearly thought that I was the sort of man who would agree to that.

I resolved to give the matter some thought and to appear in the company of the courtiers until the conspirators made the next move. I told no one of my suspicions. I could not show my hand until I knew where I stood. In truth, I was greatly troubled. Was the Empire's claim on me greater than my friendship with the king? I could not answer that question. It nagged at me.

These questions were put to me the next night, as I passed quietly along the fringes of the Autumnal Ball, held under the balmy moonlight in the winter-tinted breeze. It was likely to be one of the last good nights of the summer before the fall storms hit. Torches flickered in the gardens, and a calmer yellow light flowed over the king and queen on their dais, pouring from the Archmagus's glass globe. Revelry and merriment in the throng, plotting and whispers among the dark, assignations and threats, promises and betrayals—all the usual despicable entertainment of the court. I, of course, stuck to the shadows, fending off requests to dance with a slight smile and a gesture toward my leg: I had bandaged it earlier in the night to provide myself with an excuse to keep from dancing, and I was careful to favor it visibly.

This caution, however, was not enough to protect me from the worst injury I have received in all my time in the Imperial armies. Worse still, this injury came from one of my most trusted friends.

As I chatted amiably with Captain Hargrave, one of the king's pages found me and bade me follow her. She led me to the king's pavilion, and I entered. He sat alone, stretched out on a comfortable couch, his once-muscled frame now given way to fat. A glass of wine sat near to hand, and the remains of his dinner lay strewn on the small table in front of him. I bowed deeply; though we had been friends for decades, he was still my king.

"Your Majesty."

"Forgive me if I don't get up," he said. "Please, have a seat, have a seat."

I took a small chair, facing him. He swallowed some wine and began to tear my heart to pieces.

"We have had many years together, have we not, Glasyin? I remember best the times before the coronation. Fewer cares then, eh? Still all the interminable business of learning to be king and leading the country and so forth, but—bah. I dwell too much in the past these days, and it worries me. And that's what I wanted to speak to you about."

"I'm afraid I don't follow you."

"My faculties are slipping, General. My mind is not what it once was. Nor, I should add, is my body. I've lost much of my grace with my lack of activity." He belched. "Pardon me. I have worked long for the Empire, and I think I have done a passable job of keeping it together. We have built it well toward the future, you and I, and I think it time we began passing the work of maintaining it to a younger generation."

"Your Majesty, I—"

He interrupted me with a curt wave of his hand. "You are no longer a young man either, Glasyin. You have served with distinction and honor these many years, and our armies are in the best shape they have ever been, I believe. This is due to your leadership and your innovations. However, it is time for you to step aside and allow new vision to guide our forces."

"Your Majesty—"

"Your pension is assured, of course, and I have signed an order granting you and your heirs land in perpetuity in honor of the service you have performed for this Empire."

"Your Majesty!"

He looked me in the eye, then, and I saw some of his old fire. "General, your time is through. You are an excellent leader of men, but you are not well loved in the court. I need a commander who is equally adept at the tactics of the court as the strategy of the battlefield. To that end, I have appointed Count-General Beremany as the new leader of our forces, effective immediately."

"Your Majesty, he is a capable leader and brilliant strategist, but I do not believe he has the necessary understanding of the common soldier to—"

"What does the common soldier matter?"

"A great deal, your Majesty," I replied hotly, "if you hope to win battles!"

"Then I'm sure Beremany will learn to understand them better."

"I'm sure he'll be another butcher like Hawkins."

"Are you questioning my order, General?"

"Of course not, your Majesty, but—"

"Then I suggest you shut your mouth."

I did. An attendant came and whispered in the king's ear.

He closed his eyes. "I respect you a great deal, Glasyin, more than you imagine. I have relied on you for years to guide me true. I do not do this lightly. There are political matters at stake as well. None of our enemies can mount a credible threat to us at this point. If I thought otherwise, this would be a much harder decision. As it is, our greatest threats come from within the Empire. Do not imagine I have not felt the strain of keeping it together. The appointment of Beremany will appease a certain faction, and when the tension has eased, I will allow you to name his successor. Five to ten years should be enough."

I swallowed. "Your Majesty, may I address my troops?"

"You may. Naturally, I expect you to present this in a positive light. I know you love this land, Glasyin."

"Thank you, your Majesty."

"I'll let you make the announcement to the court tomorrow."

"Thank you." I rose.

"As you leave, please send Beremany in."

I bowed slightly, turned, and left the pavilion. Black-haired, black-hearted Jason Beremany stood outside, his handsome face wreathed with satisfaction. He bowed his head, and it was good that he did, for had I seen a smile on his face, I would have slit his throat from ear to ear.

I found Hargrave and told him to call a general muster of his troops in the morning. He opened his mouth to ask why, saw my face, and left half-running. In my turn, I retreated to a marble bench in the back of the garden. I couldn't leave the party now, but at the same time, I had no desire to be the object of everyone's gossip. I was certain Beremany had spread news of his good fortune and my ill before he even entered the pavilion. That scheming little bastard.

I sat in the dark, listening to the party, plotting, plotting. The revel was winding down when the Count of Ithan threw himself noisily to the marble bench beside me. I knew this pudgy man fairly well, and had even counted myself among the outer reaches of his circle of friends at one point. He was a vivacious, jovial man, but I knew a calculating, cunning mind lay beneath his kindness. Still and all, he was not a bad man. I liked him better than most in the court.

"What a night, Glasyin, what a night!" he exclaimed, wiping the sweat from his brow. "I've been dancing all night with anyone who'd have me."

I forced a laugh. "But for my leg, I'd have joined you myself."

"What happened?" he asked.

"A stupid accident," I replied. "While I was cleaning my dress sword, I dropped it. My reflexes are slowing. It's a good thing my mind remains as sharp as ever, because it appears that I can't be trusted to carry my own blades."

He laughed with me, but I thought his laughter had a forced quality. Perhaps I was imagining it. He leaned back, stretching, and said, "Ah, but fighting in the wars personally is no longer your duty, is it?"

"That task has fallen to more able citizens," I replied curtly.

"For the many battles you've fought, I suppose, it's only just that you can now retire safely behind the lines." He paused. "Of course, I have heard the news, and you have my condolences."

"My thanks."

"I know that the warriors of Ithan County felt safe with your steady hand guiding them in the wars. Many of the other counties' men feel the same. You are a valuable resource to this land, Glasyin. In fact, I'd say that your leadership might be all that keeps the army in line right now. Who knows what might happen with Beremany in charge?"

I turned my head to him again. He was gazing at me blandly, but I could practically hear his thoughts. I looked back at a few revelers staggering through the gardens. I turned my eyes out over the city stretched out beneath us, and said calmly, "I saw a puppet show in the city the other day."

He looked surprised, but said nothing. I continued, "I found it entertaining. All these marionettes, dancing on strings controlled by a woman hidden behind the facade. They danced and moved through their routines, through the play she'd written for them, and all the children were delighted with the show. They forgot that they were watching an artist at work and were transported by the story the puppets told. When it was over and the children left, the puppets lay on the stage, unmoving. I congratulated the puppeteer on a fine show."

He raised his eyebrows. "I'm not certain what you mean."

"Puppets are entertainment," I replied, "tools. When their strings are being manipulated, they put on a hell of a show. When they're not, they're boring, lifeless, dead. It's the puppeteer who's full of life. It's the puppeteer who's the one the crowd should get to know."

"I don't follow you."

"I'm ready to see the guiding hand behind this show," I said. "No disrespect intended, my dear count, but I have had enough of the marionettes."

He had the good sense to pretend ignorance and rose apologetically. "Ah, General," he said, "perhaps we have both had enough to drink. I wish you a good night, and hope to see you when we're a little less... well..." He bowed and smiled.

I grinned mirthlessly at him and offered no other words as he left. A good exit, I thought, and one that would cover for him should I decide to reveal the plot. I never considered the possibility that he might not be involved. Of course he was.

I reclined on the bench, closing my eyes for a few brief minutes in the predawn darkness, and I heard the click of boot heels coming down the marble walk toward me. I cracked my eyes as the walker stopped in front of me. Duke Athedon (a favored scion of House Cronen), dressed casually as usual, disdaining the finery of the court even on a formal occasion. Athedon. Beremany was in his House. A cousin, if I recalled correctly.

"Do you mind if I sit here, General Glasyin? I'd like a word or two with you." His voice was low and even, with an undercurrent of warmth.

"Regarding puppets?" I said. "Plots in the darkness and so forth?"

"Actually, yes."

"I congratulate you on your show, sir. All your puppets have performed nicely. I wasn't aware that you had strings attached to the king as well, though."

"I hope you will forgive me for that, Glasyin. I needed someone whose weaknesses I could control—a man whose nature I know well. I hope you will recognize this as a compliment to you. It's a poor strategist who commits himself without knowing the strength of all forces. I do not have your measure, but I respect you tremendously. I simply couldn't risk it."

"My thanks, Athedon, but the time for flattery has passed."

"The time for flattery should never have existed, General. So let me ask directly: Do you know what is coming?"

"I believe," I replied, "that you are planning a coup, probably before winter ends, or perhaps shortly thereafter. I have seen the positions in the palace changing. I have seen the king bow to political expediency in the name of national security. And knowing full well my loyalty to the Empire, you have removed me from the position from which I might oppose this coup."

His expression didn't move, but a smile came to his eyes. "Glasyin, I am glad to know that I did not underestimate you. I know that you are shocked and surprised to find my... our... plans so far along. I believe you to be an honorable man, and a good man, and your opinion matters more than you know. May I tell you how all this came to happen?"

I nodded, and wondered where his assassins were. He wouldn't be telling me this unless he knew perfectly well that no others could hear his treachery.

He said, "I am a student of history. I have read all the great historians of our age and the last, as well as the more obscure theoreticians and the writers of historical fiction. I have studied the ebb and flow of power from one country to the next over hundreds of years, and I have come to the inescapable conclusion that unless something dramatic happens with this land, we will lose ourselves in the mists of history. I am not talking about *eventually*, I am talking about the next generation. If we wait even another decade, it may be too late.

"Our king has sired his children in the winter of his life. He is old. He is infirm. His mind is not what it was. He is, in short, dying. His new wife is a scheming, power-mad shrew who cannot be trusted, and who focuses on trivial slights. He married her to strengthen his position with the High Houses. He does not trust her, and because she is a Bhumar, neither do the others. In fact, none will accept her as regent, and the civil war that will result in her ascension will tear our provinces apart."

It was true what he said. It was an open secret that Bhumar was heavily invested in the underworld, and if they did not break Imperial law daily, they surely danced upon the line. Yet they brought money to the treasury and helped the Empire pay its bills, and the House spies and informants would have surely proven useful. Yet here I sat, next to the man who had made all those spies useless, and I could not help but agree with his assessment.

"I love this land, Glasyin. I love what we have become. But unless we receive fresh blood and new leadership, all that we have worked for and all that our forefathers achieved will be lost to time. I am not yet willing to let that go. Are you?"

"You're asking me to choose between my oldest friend and the land I love."

"Yes, I am. I am aware of what I'm asking, and I realize that it is a horrible choice."

"The betrayal of my friendship or the betrayal of my duty."

"Yes. But keep in mind that your friend has betrayed you, sacrificing you to ease strain on himself."

"A betrayal you engineered."

"It was a test for him as well, Glasyin. Had he stood fast, you and I would not be having this discussion. I do not think I have misjudged you. I think that you recognize the necessity of sacrifice. Your entire career has hinged around the understanding of this most difficult reality."

We sat in silence for a while. The sky began to brighten with the predawn, roseate tinges breaking the relentless grip of night.

I said at last, "You have done me a great disservice. You have treated the king unjustly."

Athedon snorted. "Loyalty and justice are opposites. Surely you realized this! You cannot serve a man and serve an ideal at the same time. Men die. But a civilization can last many years longer. You are at the linchpin of the Empire's history right now, General, and you must make your decision. I must insist on it."

"Answer this one question for me, then."

"Absolutely. Whatever I can tell you."

"Who will rule in Fannon's place? And what shall become of him and his children?"

"You're not asking where your place is in this?" he asked.

"I already know. I too have studied history, Athedon. Let me outline exactly how this falls out: when my... my *former* staff comes to me to ask my advice and possibly my leadership, for they will not trust Beremany, I will inform them that I accept you and yours as the new rulers. I will suggest that they do the same for the good of the Empire. The army then stays out of the coming battles. And then, for me, an honorable exile."

"That is what I anticipated," he replied equably.

"You won't be able to trust me if I agree to this." I held up a hand as he began to protest. "If I take a position against my old friend, that shows that

I can be leveraged with a threat to our nation. If I do not take that position, I am giving up the oath I swore to protect the Empire. Either way, I break faith. As I said, you have done me a grave disservice. I know what happens to oathbreakers and traitors."

"Glasyin, I would hold you in the highest esteem. I would not allow any to cast doubt or blame on you." He kept his gaze steady on mine as he said this. I decided that he was lying, and I think that may have been the moment I made my decision.

"In exchange for this," I said, "you will allow me to name my successor. I would not have that smirking toad Beremany leading my forces to war. I think he would kill too many of our men because he does not value them."

He frowned. "I owe my cousin several favors. This appointment was to have wiped the slate clean."

"That is my price. That, and the knowledge of what you intend to do with Fannon and his family."

He sighed and looked to the sky. "Exile. We would need to take the king and his family someplace far away, where they could not build an army of loyalists to restore themselves to power. I love the old man, too, you know. You are not the only person who has a history with him. I would not see him suffer. I wish him no harm."

"And our new ruler?"

He glanced down at his hands. "I have done the hard work of organizing this. I understand the course of history. I intend for the Empire to survive the coming years. As the man who brought us this far, as the man with the vision to see that it must be done, I believe that I am the one best suited to lead us."

"Of course, of course." The sun began to crest the peaks on the far side of the Carrerel Range. "How do you intend to deal with the Knights Elite?"

"I have planned for that as well. I flatter myself by imagining that I have a plan for nearly any eventuality. You are at one of the decision points right now. I need an answer so I know which strategy moves forward."

"May I give you my answer tomorrow morning?"

"You are one of my key elements. By revealing my plans to you, since they are months from fruition and can still be stopped, you become a danger. I need to know where you stand."

"You have given me much to think about. You know that I do nothing rashly."

He looked inward and nodded toward the rising sun. "Are you sure it cannot be this morning?"

"Yes."

"Very well. Think deeply, sir. I am certain that you will come to the proper answer. Should you realize the right path, send a courier today." He rose, turned, and gave me a slight bow. "It has been my pleasure, Glasyin. I do apologize for all that has happened, and all that is to come."

I waited a few moments after he departed. By the gods! Where were the Imperial spies in this? Where were the High Houses? Where, indeed, were the Lesser Houses? Athedon had been thorough indeed. How long had he been planning this, truly? It must have been well before the king began his dotage. I could not help but think that he had been plotting his treason for at least a decade to have so many of these pieces in place. There was nothing honorable in this. His concern for the Empire was a cover. Thus decided, I rose to stretch.

As I did, I felt a presence behind me. I cursed inwardly and scrabbled for my blade, trying to turn quickly enough to dodge the inevitable killing blow. Of course Athedon had taken even this small delay as refusal! Even as I turned, I imagined the knife slicing my throat open.

Instead I saw one of the younger Knights Elite standing back, his gauntleted hands held before him, empty. "My apologies for surprising you, sir, and I'd appreciate if you didn't draw your weapon on me. My conditioning might kill you."

My reflexes were fast enough to loose the hilt before the sword was halfway from its sheath, and it slid, hissing, back into the scabbard. "Sir Knight, you gave me a hell of a scare." I thought, at first, he might be a witness, that he could help me to expose this plot.

"Pelagir, sir. Knight of the Order Elite, Class of the Crown." I studied him. Dark hair. Dark eyes. Strong, lean frame. Formal armor. And, of course, the cool, dead eyes and dispassionate voice of the Knights Elite.

"Of course. I have seen you guarding the king. What can I do for you?"

With his order's bluntness, he said, "Accept his offer."

"What?"

"I said to accept the duke's offer. It may not be too late. You have my utmost respect, General Glasyin, but if you do not accept his offer now, you will be dead before the sun rises tomorrow."

I chuckled. "So the king is still watching, is he? And he wants an agent in the duke's camp?"

"The king is not watching. The king is as good as dead. The focus of his spies is scattered, like light through a prism. They have no direction. The duke's plan is the Empire's only hope."

I was shocked to the core. "I thought the oaths of the knights were unbreakable!"

"The oath I took in initiation is to the security of the Empire. I have seen the king's fallibility."

"How did they turn you?"

He frowned. "I have not turned. I have seen that there is no loyalty to us from above. Without loyalty above, there can be no true service below. General, I have no more time to talk to you. Great events are in the making. You can stand with us at the wheel of history, or you can be crushed by it. Your time is running out. I hope you will make the wiser choice." He turned and moved quickly toward the palace doors.

I returned immediately to my room and gathered my most important effects: papers and money, for my seals will be useless and my clothes will scream my identity. I have found this inn, and I have been writing all day. I intend to depart tonight, cloaked and disguised, and will entrust these pages to a friend in the city if I am certain I have not been followed. I must ready myself for the journey I have put off for too long. I shall leave Terona, most likely for the last time. They will have noticed my absence in the palace, but will likely have put it down to conferring with advisors and preparing the transition of command. No one knows where I am now.

I do not believe Terona will survive the storm that rides on the heels of this autumn rain. After a life of decision, I am presented with a dilemma that I cannot break. I cannot betray my friend as he has betrayed me. I do not know if I could alter events even if I chose to. I cannot make this decision, not even for the sake of the Empire. I cannot make it for Athedon, a blandly ambitious man who would lie to my face for his own gain. After the sudden shock of having my command stripped and my identity as a leader torn apart in a single night, I do not have it in me. I hope that others will resist him better than I can.

I flee for my life and for my honor, but in truth, I am weary of the endless politicking, the lies and slanders, the needless outrages so that one faction may gain a slight advantage over another. When betrayal is the grease that keeps the wheel of Empire turning, I can no longer remain within its cycles. Our Empire is sick. I know the cancer that lies at its heart. I do not believe we will recover.

The time is past midnight now.

There is a knocking at my door. It must be a word from one of my lieutenants. I had not thought they would come so quickly.

They have underestimated me. It is certainly not the first time. Let us hope it is not the last. My assassin is dead and I live, though with a wound that will take some time to heal. Athedon did not even respect me enough to send one of his traitor knights for me. Who was that man? He was barely at the level of a household guard. Their mistake, and my blessing. Once again, I am glad of my wrist knife. I suppose I should also be grateful for having thought to bandage myself to escape the dance. They must have thought I'd move more slowly than I did. Sometimes, I suppose, the little details in our lives mean the most.

Was I tracked to this place? Who betrayed me? Was it Hargrave? Westkitt? M'Cray? All my dreams of mustering a resistance to this coup are dust. If I cannot trust even those three, who will follow me? Whom shall I lead? No. I must flee the city and slink into exile.

There can be no hope for the king. I pray that his children will survive. I do not think there is any hope, but I pray that I am wrong.
I bid you farewell, my home. I weep for you. The storm outside howls its grief with me.

Interlude: Out of the City

Pelagir bent low across the neck of his steed and whispered into its steel ear. The machine leapt forward, streaking across the farmland. He shot a glance behind him and saw the city in flames. His doing, he thought, and perhaps his undoing. But then . . . he looked down at his bundle, the baby girl, and his jaw hardened. He had made his choices. He carried the future. He bore the princess Caitrona, by now surely the last of her line. He was headed for the King's Forest. Miles of countryside and farms stretched ahead of him, interrupted here and there by towns and hamlets: Knollside, Warsend, Colm, Highridge Glen, and more, strung like drab jewels along the roads. The sun settled ahead of him as the city burned behind.

Year 1 – CY 578

Pelagir's first year of training was not turning out as he thought it might.

The freedom of which he had dreamed during nights in bed at home had been replaced with a harsher discipline. He lay in the darkness of the high-ceilinged dormitory with the west wind overturning the peace of the night outside, and he thought of the endless days ahead of him echoing the days he had left behind: days of standing motionless under the hot sun and cold rain, days of menial chores, days of backbreaking weapons work, days and days and days and days. This was not freedom. This was slavery, and toward what goal? Service. Service to fat men making stupid decisions, and he would be expected to rectify their mistakes with blood. He had sold himself to death at an enemy's hand, or at the executioner's, or the little death of disgrace. He had traded his father for the people who had created his father.

He thought he had buried his heart long ago, but now he discovered it bleeding on the pillow beside him, and he wept bitter tears—bitter but quiet, because showing emotion was punishable by a morning whipping.

When he awoke, his pillow was wet, and they took him to the courtyard and whipped him in front of the other students. And then they sent him to stand in heavy armor in the hot sun for the day.

It was one day among hundreds. The trainers drove their students mercilessly, and this first year was constant marching, drills, hand-to-hand exercises, and training in basic weapons. Those who complained or broke were beaten, as Pelagir had been, and some of them died between the whipping posts. No one was allowed to mourn the dead.

Year 2 – CY 579

Pelagir's second year of training was little better. The discipline was harsher, his instructors less forgiving, and his training more dangerous than the year before. He bore scars from lashings for failure to obey—or remember—the rules or the Code. It was better for him than for many of his compatriots. Two thousand youths had been gathered from all the reaches of the Empire, and half of them had been expelled for one reason or another. Some of them had died. They were fourteen years of age.

Those who remained were harder, stronger. They studied harder and learned faster. They understood that it was not their bodies and minds being tested but their dedication. Most of them would fail and fall into a lesser position in the military. Some would serve in the High House to which their family swore loyalty. Others might become mercenaries. They would be tougher than many of their conventionally trained counterparts, but they would live with the knowledge that they had failed the knighthood. Some, armed with this insight, took their own lives.

Pelagir didn't have time to give them a second thought. He was trying to survive.

This year, amid the constant training in arms of all shapes and sizes, he learned Imperial history: the mythical Golden Age, an age of casual miracles and everyday wonders, and its fall. The horrific and destructive war, and the wonder-workers called "scientists" who fled to strong men for protection from the rabble who blamed deep knowledge for the destruction of the Age. This was the Great Uprising. More war, and the terrors of wizardry truly unleashed as the mages worked to save their lords from their enemies, earning a greater place in the nightmares of the common folk. Generations of struggle as small men fought with one another to make large their dreams, and from these small men at last rose a great man: Martyn Strangaers, our first king, who had the charisma, wit, and will necessary to bring the warring lords under his control. He established a central government in the hilly town of Terona, his birthplace, and with his warlords at his side and his pet wizard at his back, he began to subjugate the lands around his hometown. By the time of his death, he sat on the throne of empire and had rebuilt civilization, dragging it screaming from the dark age that had settled upon the land.

As a broad stroke, this was all essentially correct. It was in the details that this history was wrong, but it was wrong for a purpose: it helped fill the young knights with devotion for the Empire they were sworn to defend.

That devotion came with the Code, ritually repeated, used as a marching cadence, as a breathing exercise, fit into every corner and cranny of their waking minds. At first they hated the Code, but they grew to rely on it as the sole touchstone in their training that never changed. They could recite it in their sleep.

"Honor is strength. Honor is integrity. Honor is dedication. My life is my honor, my honor my life. I value my honor more highly."

And another oath, as well:

"I am the stone on which my order rests. My order is the stone on which the knighthood rests. The knighthood is the stone on which the realm rests. I am stone, and when I stand fast, so too does the realm. If I fail, the realm fails. I am its defender. My commitment never dies.

"I am the steel of my country. I do not bend. I will not break."

Year 3 – CY 580

By his third year, three hundred of his classmates remained. Half of them would go on to the Knights Lesser. Many of the remainder would go to the ranks of the Knights Faithful. A select handful would achieve the honor of Knight Elite. Only ten such slots were available per year, and they were not filled if too few candidates were suitable. The competition was fierce. Though the students had been trained against desire, they sought honor, and the greatest honor and glory would belong to those who belonged in turn to the Empire, body and soul.

Pelagir had learned to crush his expectations and deal with immediate necessity. He could forecast, anticipate, and plan for eventualities, and he had one of the finest minds among the students of his year—indeed, of any class in the school that year. Further, the lessons they had taught him in this year had been successful in driving hope from his spirit. He planned, he improvised, and he did not hope. He trusted to his training and his ability to carry him through, but he shed no tears if he failed. This culling of his spirit, his native intelligence, and his stoicism in the face of pain and humiliation made him eligible for the rank of Elite.

This also made Pelagir a target of his classmates. Though the students were forbidden to kill or maim one another, their instructors tacitly encouraged the harshest possible competition. They believed that the smarter and stronger students would be best served by cultivating paranoia, remaining wary for traps and betrayals at all times, and that the lesser students would learn to work together to bring down the leaders. Their traps fell into a variety of categories, but these physical and mental gambits often were complete failures and occasionally were disasters. The other candidates, male or female, though intelligent, were not in the class of their superiors, and their efforts sometimes rebounded on them, with deadly results. When at last they realized they were completely outmatched by the better students, the lesser students rejected all contact with them, and this was the most effective betrayal of all.

Worse yet, the best candidates couldn't trust one another. They were in competition for the ten Elite slots, so they met with their peers only on the practice field and in the classrooms, where they struggled to prove themselves in the eyes of instructors. They were otherwise in almost total isolation.

This, too, was planned. It had been the custom for hundreds of years.

Year 4 – CY 581

Two hundred students. Of the hundred missing, twenty-six had died. Sixty-one had tested out early to squirehood in the Knights Lesser. Thirteen had been withdrawn by their families—though difficult, it was possible, especially in the case of students with no prospects in the knighthood. Those thirteen might do well in the regular armed forces, but they would always recognize their failure to enter the knighthood.

One hundred seventy-three of the remainder were destined for the Knights Faithful, and their work now determined their rank within the order on graduation. The last twenty-seven were in competition for the ten Elite spots, and nobles from the great families came to watch them in training. The candidates who failed to achieve Elite status were automatically part of the high ranks of the Knights Faithful, valuable recruits, and the Houses of the Empire paid well for their services. The Knights Elite were answerable only to the king and those he chose to speak for him, performing the tasks necessary to maintain the Empire, but the other orders traveled among the Houses, every two years delivered by dirigible to those who had asked for their aid. They returned to Terona at the end of their term for training in the rugged terrain to the north of the city, and as long as the Houses paid their leases, the Houses retained the services of highly trained and most deadly warriors. The knights' loyalty was to the Empire first, to their brotherhood second, and to their adopted Houses last, so when no external threats materialized, they fought against one another in the many internecine battles between Houses great and small.

This mattered little to the young men and women who sought the slots. The knighthood's regimen had driven ordinary ambition and emotion from them. They struggled now against one another, a competition among near-equals, for their place in legend. They believed that if they could achieve Elite, their struggles would be against the heroes of the past. For now, though, they trained, they studied, they marched hard miles under the blazing sun and under the torrential mountain rains. They fought in muddy trenches, across fields strewn with mountains of dirt and shreds of metal. They trained with swords and spears, bows and siege engines, and other, more esoteric devices created by the Archmagus and his acolytes. They spent a month alone in the wilderness, living off nothing but their wits

Through it all, they were observed by a cadre of Knights Elite, to whom the duty of training this raw flesh would fall. Pelagir's witness, Lieutenant Caltash, took a special interest in his charge and set him a variety of tests to gauge the boy's reactions. Caltash liked what he found. He liked it very much indeed.

At the end of the fourth year, one of ten. This letter went to the Knight Assessors, who oversaw the training and advancement of the young candidates:

By order of the Commander of Knights Assembled,
On this, the third day of the month of the Eagle, of the year Crystal, of the cycle Strength, commonly known as the 581st Clasping Year, let it be known that Pelagir Amons has surpassed our expectations. Let it be known that he has been judged and found worthy. Let him be borne away to Devilsfoot on this night. Let him be delivered to the tower of the Archmagus, where he shall undergo his final excruciations. Let him receive a blood weapon of his choosing. Let him be admitted into the sacred brotherhood of the Knights Elite. Let him give the remaining portion of his life in service to the Empire.

To this I set my seal.

<signed>
Sir Ellionn Carderas, Commander of the Knights Assembled, Duke
of the Eastern Protectorate, Earl of Farassi, Viscount of Hanging Bay,
Baron of Suthersford

The walls of the King's Forest loomed ahead of him, tall trees planted
firmly across hundreds of rolling acres. Pelagir pulled back on the reins and
dismounted, sliding from the saddle in a single fluid motion. From his pouch he
extracted a flask of milk and set it to the child's lips. She drank thirstily, burped
once, and fell asleep. Pelagir laid a blanket on the ground, set her gently on it,
and set about making the modifications to his steed that would help him hide
his trail. Inside the wood the King's Foresters patrolled. If he wasn't careful,
their snares could undo him.

He bent to his work.

THE FORESTER'S TALE

Cold steel presses into my throat, and passionless eyes stare into mine. My death is upon me... but I feel no fear. The woods are alive around me. I hear birds call, and the hum of the forest's insects is a reassuring drone. The afternoon's rain drips from the leaves, and the setting sun sparkles through the trees like an oaken halo. I am not afraid to die in the woods I love.

All morning we were on full alert—we, the elite of the King's Foresters, knew this forest better than our husbands and wives and children, better than we knew each other, better than our most intimate lovers. The forest nurtures us, fills us with joy, breathes new hope into lives dulled by pain, war, suffering. We are renewed here. In the wind's whispering tracks we hear the health of the river that nourishes the mighty trees. The forest is our home.

We were alert before Cox summoned us to the lodge with three short blasts on his horn—the breeze broke in strange ways that morning, and the birds screamed their indignation from their high nests: the forest's peace was broken by an intruder. We knew the intruder was alone. We knew he was skilled in the lore of our wood, too, because we didn't know where he was.

We also knew he was dangerous. Cox would never have called us otherwise. He would have let us track the intruder down ourselves and deal with the interloper as we dealt with all trespassers in the King's Forest. We showed no mercy.

We gathered at the stilt lodge, moving silently, singly and in pairs among the old trunks. Usually we traveled alone, but this was the Year of the Journeyman. Those of us who had taken 'prentices two years ago now traveled with our charges to see their skills. Warren had Xis, an old southern infantryman who had taken to the teachings as well as any child, and already he moved more silently than some who had been born to the wood. Three others came as well, with the nicknames we'd given 'em: Toll Halfman, the eunuch from Terona; Strom Surehand from the cold northeast; and Brus the Clean.

My 'prentice had washed out. There was no shame in it.

I was one of the first to arrive. We greeted each other with a nod and a name ("Mishi," they said to me), and no more—foresters are quiet folk at the best of times. When thirty of us were there, Cox began to speak. His words were terse, clipped. "I received word from Terona. The intruder is one of the King's Chosen. His name is Pelagir. He's carrying a child. If the child comes to harm, it'll be your head. The Council of Knights has asked that we shoot to wound Pelagir, not to kill him. Recovery of the child is of primary importance."

It meant a kidnapping, then, from a family high up the social ladder. Maybe the highest. The Council wanted vengeance, and it was going to be terrible. We'd pay if we stood in the way of their punishment. And if we had to die to get the child, it wasn't sacrifice enough.

We slung our yew bows onto the pegs in the walls and took the dull bronze crossbows from the racks in their place—plain arrows wouldn't do against one of the King's Chosen. There was no way we could fire an arrow that would hit him unless we managed a distraction, and that was unlikely. True, the crossbows were unreliable. Sometimes they exploded when they fired, sometimes they didn't fire at all, and they required yearly maintenance by Verthain, the wizard of the forest. But against a knight, the eldritch bolts they fired were the best option we had. These crossbows had no strings to tangle in the brushes and branches. The forks summoned and focused energy from within the worked metal of the weapon, launching the quarrel only when we squeezed the crossbow's stock. If they were more trustworthy, we'd use them all the time. As it was, we used the yew bows except in emergencies. If worse slipped to worst, we had our knives, though of course they'd be useless against a knight.

We left the stilt lodge without saying anything else and fanned out through the woods to the west. If we ran across the knight, we'd be dead unless we had backup, but we couldn't travel too closely together, or he'd be warned of our coming. Against any ordinary person, these precautions would have been unnecessary. We'd use these tactics against one of the vicious things that sometimes wandered into the forest from the blasted hills, and the cautions would keep us safe. Against one of the King's Chosen, they might not be enough.

I grew afraid then—afraid of losing the forest, afraid of losing my life. My heart knocked in my chest, and my legs weakened as I trotted through the massive trunks. But my only choices were to pursue the knight and the child, or to break my oath and lose my life. In the end, I had no choice at all. I would die in the service of the forest I swore to protect.

That didn't diminish my fear in the slightest.

I slipped through the underbrush, the crossbow fastened tight against my back. I ducked hanging branches and leaped over fallen trees. I launched myself over moss-laden rocks, grasping vines that hung from the high branches. I called out in birdsong as I ran and heard trills from the other foresters. We spread farther and farther apart as the hours wore on, and still we came across no sign of Pelagir.

It was midafternoon. We had been running for most of the day and still had no sign of the knight, no warning from the others. I'd come across Strom's trail, and hooted thrice to let him know I'd seen it. His master Karl would want to know. Clouds had built in the sky since the morning, and a cold wind rushed through the forest, swaying the trees and stripping leaves from their branches. I knew the signs of the storm. This was going to be a loud one.

When it broke, it broke hard. The lightning tore into the day's gloom, the thunder following in a swift counterstroke, the sign for the rain to fall on us like heaven's arrows. For a less experienced forester, this would wipe out all traces of Pelagir's passing. Not for us.

I covered my crossbow with a sheet of brown felt to protect it from the rain and set out again, choosing my steps with greater care. It wouldn't do to slip now. I cast my eyes more carefully along the forest floor. I watched for any sign out of the ordinary, and found none. I called out in birdsong again to see if any of the other foresters could hear me over the rain and thunder. I waited for a minute and called again. I tightened the crossbow's strap and wove south and westward through the wood.

I stopped at the first sight of blood on the northern banks of the Branish River. The splatter was already nearly lost in the rain. I unslung my crossbow and started to run along the bloody trail.

It grew fresher as I ran. I had forgotten my fear in the run through the forest, but now it returned full force. I smelled death in the air.

I rounded a bend in the river's course and saw Xis stretched out on the pebbles by the water's edge. His soft leather jerkin had a hole about the size of my fist in the middle of his chest, darkening red against his dark skin. His blood pumped rich and scarlet into the water. I trotted to him, cautious of ambush. I lifted his head gently.

"Xis..."

"Mishi," he whispered, and coughed blood. "Warren did't. Had a clear shot, he jogged my arm. Fought. Sliced him. Fled. Shot me here. Dying. Hurts."

I kissed his eyes, farewell forester-style, and opened the big vein in his throat with my belt knife. I watched in respect until he stopped breathing. The rain slipped into slight drizzle, soon headed for mist, and the clouds began to break in the few moments it took. I checked his crossbow. It was ruined, and I left it with his body. I fired a single shot from mine into the air, a signal flare for the others. I marked five stones to point where I'd gone, and I ran, ran. I was more afraid than ever.

Warren, a traitor. Who knew how many more of our kind Pelagir had under his spell? I had known Warren for years. He had always seemed loyal. Now I was facing a forester as skilled as I was, and a knight to boot. My heart sank. I knew I wouldn't leave the day alive.

Warren was close, I knew. He hadn't taken the time to bind his wound. He was running alone on the river's edge, bleeding. It was a stupid mistake...

... or was it? I stopped. I crept back into the cover of the hilly woods and started looking. In a few moments, I saw him.

Warren was pressed against the bole of a huge oak tree, sighting down his crossbow atme. I raised my weapon, knowing it was already too late, when he flung his bow to the ground with a curse and rushed at me. He drew his knife as he came, and I could not understand his shouts or the look of panic in his eyes.

I fired once, and the impact took him off his feet. I think I got him in the head. I watched him fall for an instant.

Something heavy slammed into me from behind. My head hit a trunk on the way down. Darkness rushed into my eyes as earth filled my mouth.

When I opened my eyes, my back was to a tree, my arse on the ground. There was a blade at my throat. Behind that knife was the man I'm looking for, hoping not to find. And behind that man stood death. My fear surged into my throat. Just as quickly, it slipped from me like a waterfall.

I am fully in the moment of my life and my death.

"Pelagir," I say.

"Forester. How many of you follow me today? How soon can I expect them?"

"How long was I unconscious?"

"A minute and a half."

"You probably have five minutes. You might be able to escape in time." No use in lying.

"I might. It was a pity you shot your friend." For the first time, I hear something in his voice. Compassion, perhaps?

"Xis said he was a traitor. Said Warren jogged his arm and then shot him."

His hard mouth quirks slightly. "It was the other way around. Xis was a friend of mine in the eastern war. When he heard my name today, he thought he would repay a debt. Your friend Warren did much better in close quarters against a soldier than I'd have given a forester credit for. But Xis gave me time to get off the river. Is he dead?"

I think of lying this time. But then I realize it won't matter—he'll kill me fast either way. "Yes. I slit a vein. There was no helping him.

Where is the child?"

"In a safe place. She's sleeping." The light dims from his eyes. "Will you renounce your oath and let me go free? Or do you die here?"

"I die today one way or another, from you or my fellows. If I let you go, I would live only another few minutes."

"I have no taste for killing women who perform their duty faithfully, forester. I've seen and done enough of that in the city."

"You've broken *your* oath, Sir Pelagir. Why do you care about morals now?"

Now I see actual hurt in his eyes. "Mine required me to be faithless. I could not bear it any longer." The knife presses harder. "But I have no more time to exchange words. I ask one last time: Will you let us flee? Will you help lay a false trail?"

I look beyond him at the squirrels dancing on the branches of the trees. Tears spring unbidden to my eyes.

I take in what might be my final breath.

"No."

The knife leaves my throat for a second. The clouds break behind the knight as he brings his knife back for a swing. Through my tears, the sun shines golden behind his head.

He reverses his dagger at the far end of the arc, and the pommel crashes into my temple. Darkness comes, and surprised gratitude is the last light I see that day. I must face the judgment of my fellows, but I am breathing even as I slip into unconsciousness.

The Tale of the Excruciations

Morning, early spring, and the chill had not yet left the air. The courser's motion was smooth, even as it leaped rocks, streams, logs. Pelagir sat atop his mount, cradling the child. His face was dirty with the dust of the countryside.

Spring, Month of the Metal Dog, CY 581

The dormitory of the senior squires was quiet, moonlight from the high windows streaking across the midnight floor. The boys and girls slept in their bunks, some snoring softly. A spring breeze sighed in the open windows behind the moon, and on the back of the breeze came the hooded men. There were twenty of them, and they moved without sound as they clambered through the windows. They dropped to the floor, and in teams of two they spread across the bedchamber. They took their positions, and at once, they struck.

Seven boys and three girls were clubbed, gagged, and stuffed into black sacks within moments. The twenty men and their burdens were out of the room with such efficiency that none of the other squires had awakened.

Their destination was Devilsfoot. They were to begin the excruciations.

Pelagir awoke draped unceremoniously across a saddle, and he could feel the courser moving smoothly underneath him. Its smooth gait told him that it was no natural beast. This likewise told him he was in the custody of a high-ranking officer of the Empire, which in turn suggested any attempt at escape would be noticed and dealt with harshly. Furthermore, he deduced, those squires who had made it to the fourth year—and with a record like his, no less—would be among the most carefully guarded assets of the military, and therefore he was one of the ten squires to have been chosen for the Elite. Thus it was that, like so many who had come before him, he was borne unprotesting and unresisting into Devilsfoot. Thus it was that he came to the place where the humanity had been torn from so many of his predecessors.

Like the other recruits, Pelagir was blessed and cursed with a memory that rarely failed him. Yet had he been pressed on the matter, he would never have been able to give a clear account of his time in Devilsfoot. The ride to the ancient cavern was brief, not more than twenty to thirty minutes from the dormitory, yet he had never seen the place before.

His first impression was of the sound, muffled through the heavy sack that covered him. The open air through which they had ridden suddenly became much closer, and the hooves of the metal steeds began to echo from stone walls. The air became warmer, and then hot. At last the coursers halted, and the ten squires, still in their sacks, were pitched to the rough stone floor. A quiet susurrus of clothes, then, as of robed men moving toward them, and a slight clatter as the steel steeds rode back out. And for the first time that night, voices.

"These kids get heavier every year. Are they feeding 'em more meat or something?"

"I dunno, but you're right. They're building 'em solid these days."

"We should install tracks here, put in some carts, something."

A third voice, drier: "Or maybe the two of you are just getting old. Stop complaining and pick one of 'em up... and the rest of you, stop dawdling."

Rough hands, then, and hot breath through the sack: "I know you're awake, boy, so mark me well: rest while you can, because you'll need your strength."

The hands on Pelagir then were the kindest he felt for five days.

Images of an excruciation:

First come the rituals. The ten, strapped naked to cold steel tables and wheeled under bright lights. In the darkness beyond, an amphitheater and the murmurs of dozens of students. The Archmagus donning a horned mask, black velvet filigreed in white gold and jewels. Ceremonial words in an arcane tongue pour from the Archmagus, delivered in a monotone, and the responses of the students in the shadows. It is a calming intonation, a call-response-call rhythm that soothes and focuses, but the young squires on the table are terrified beneath their carefully impassive faces. The Archmagus's students, his mages-in-training, file down the stairs and take up the instruments that lie on cloth-covered carts near each of the knights-to-be. Priests wait in the corners, their heads bowed, waiting the call to grant the final blessings on souls departing.

And then: blood. Pain. Steel.

Pelagir's arm, strapped to the table, stripped to the bone, and scalpels moving above it like fireflies. Tiny troughs funneling molten metal into cast channels along his tendons and muscles.

Agony.

Legs, feet, arms, neck. His face. His eyes. Screams from nearby tables. Anguish pours. His throat has torn. He can feel metal wires being affixed to his muscles, anchored to his bones.

The eyes of the Archmagus through the holes in the man's mask. They glitter with joy above the bloodstained face and gloves. His apprentices, who rush through the chamber.

Through it all, the quiet, murmured chanting of the apprentices and the quiet sound of metal on flesh. The priests begin to move, looking into his eyes, then the eyes of the others.

The ceiling of the cavern, the lights beaming down, halos around the heads of the surgeons. Pelagir has moved beyond pain and into a hazy realm. He watches the movements of the Archmagus as a detached observer now, watching the man's hands move surely through the violations of his body. Each second the young man chooses to live or die, and each second he chooses life. Each choice is an act of will, each one harder than the next.

The Archmagus's hands, inside his skin, manipulating him. His fingers jerking open and closed. His legs twitching. Sutures and bandages, soaking through with a deep crimson.

The chamber quiets. At two of the other tables, legs drum out a final beat as their owners succumb. From the seven remaining, Pelagir hears quiet and rasping moans. The Archmagus's apprentices wheel their patients from the room. The priests murmur their benedictions above the bodies of the dead and depart.

Behind them, pools of blood glisten wetly under the lights. Shiny metallic things crawl from slats behind the walls and suck these pools efficiently from the floor, then scurry back to their holes to await the next experiments.

And then came the graduations.

The first was private, and hardly a ceremony, held in the recovery room of the Tower of the Archmagus, one week after the ordeal. It was a dim room, with shutters on the high windows and a stout oak door at the head of the stairs. The eight young knights could hear the wind and birds outside with incredible clarity, and even the soft lights mounted high above them seemed almost too bright for comfort.

The new knights were healing quickly, far more quickly than they had ever seen their bodies heal before. They had been ordered to remain in their beds for a week by Lieutenant Caltash, who had appeared in his shining armor before his new compatriots. He kept his helmet tucked under his arm as he delivered this order, and the cast of his face brooked no dispute. He took no questions as he stepped about the room inspecting the wounded, but he did place a mailed hand on each shoulder in welcome before he left, and he gripped Pelagir's a little harder than the rest. And he told them two secrets:

"You are no longer competitors. You are companions. Look into yourselves and find the lessons the pain has taught you. You have been bound together in pain, and you are now entwined. Your old lives have fallen away.

You are new beings now, and what came before is dust. You are no longer human, and your kind exists only in the knighthood. Remember this when humans try to oppose you.

"Your second secret is this: you have gifts within you that you will discover, yet behind all those gifts, you will find joy only in dealing death. Since you have survived the excruciation, your human emotions have been buried deep within you. Should you try to recover them, you will surely die."

The lieutenant left the knights to their silence, and they began to talk among themselves shortly thereafter, as he knew they would.

The second graduation came at the expiration of the week, when the Archmagus himself came to their room, trailed by a pair of magi. The Archmagus was a wiry man with wiry hair, black and shot through with strips of iron. He wore a steel, grilled mask across the lower portion of his face—vanity, it was said, a cover for the horrific burns he had received while defending the tower on Clarkeshill from the sky reavers—and over it his hard, calculating eyes shone at the newly minted knights.

"You are more than human now. More than us. Through my art and my craft, you are faster, stronger, and you heal more quickly. You have been enhanced, from bone to muscle to sinew. Your eyesight and hearing have likewise been improved. We have done this for you, as we have done for your chapter since the founding of the Empire. Because of us, you have entered into the halls of the legends. Because we have done this for you, you will remember us. You will remember that your first loyalty is to the Empire. Your second is to your commander. But remember by all you hold dear that your third loyalty is to the Guild of the Magi, for without us you would be merely human.

"You can get out of bed now," he said. "Your commander is coming to see you, get the measure of the new improvements. I want you standing for him, and you'll want to be used to your abilities before he comes."

The Archmagus turned, paused, and turned back. "One more thing. Tell my apprentice Trellaise what sort of weapon you prefer. She will make one specifically for you, and it shall become your salvation."

He swept from the room, and that was their second graduation.

The third came a week past that. They had been exercising their new abilities (under close observation from their commanders and from the magi who had operated on them) during this week, sparring with one another, and testing their limits—by catching arrows, among other things. It had taken them some time to adjust to their hugely advanced strength and speed. At first, they fell frequently, but they quickly learned to balance themselves. They moved in a near-constant blur until Trellaise informed them that such movement reduced their healing factor and would eventually place such strain on them that their sinews might snap, which would require an operation similar to the excruciation to repair them. They began practicing ordinary movement immediately.

Then Michael Fellsfield broke his arm throwing a boulder as large as his torso, which prompted another angry rebuke. They were informed that though they were strong, they should give their bones time to adjust to these new muscles, and work their way up to such feats. Michael (who the others called "the Fortunate") was given a tight dressing to ensure the bone knitted properly; there was no splint, and he was healed before the week was through. In the meantime, the others trained fervently in order to speed the adjustment.

Of the eight, Kelvin was the most charismatic, Michael the most adventurous, Tarrason the most ambitious, and Allan the most naturally talented. Kildare was the strongest, though not by much, Sonia the fastest, and Lyral the brightest. Pelagir was strong and fast and bright, too, but his talent lay in the nearly bottomless reservoir of endurance—or possibly obstinacy—that his father had built unwittingly.

But as talented as these new knights were, something inside of them had broken during the excruciation, as it had broken for all those before them. Neither did they cry or show emotion of any sort. Where before they were tough, now they were hard and empty.

They barely noticed what they had given away.

Caltash came among them then, with others of the Elite, and they trained the newcomers to marry their speed with their minds, and of secret techniques in unarmed combat. Each of them, Caltash said, would develop a unique fighting style; these new techniques would provide a cornerstone for each style. By the time of the final graduation, a month later, the newest Elite had developed formidable killing talents.

Their final graduation, then, was an actual ceremony, an induction into the Fellowship of Knights Assembled. The ceremony took place in the vast courtyard of the Knights' Hall in the Imperial Palace, and half the knighthood was in attendance.

It was a bright blue day, and errant gusts snapped the pennons on the grandstand. The commander, Sir Ellionn Carderas, stood atop the podium, gazing with sharp eye upon all the knights of Pelagir's class who marched before him: the Lesser, the Faithful, and the Elite. They gleamed in their armor, and their feet beat a thunderous cadence on the hard-packed ground. They formed into neat rows before the dais and stood at military attention as he spoke to them of duty, honor, and their service to the Empire.

And then he called forth the newest of the Elite. They came and stood directly in front of him as attendants placed slim boxes behind the commander. Carderas unlatched the first case and reverently lifted out a gleaming metal spear. Hints of red glittered from it in the sun, chasing each other up and down the shaft. The commander held it aloft, letting the assembled warriors view it, and called out, "Sir Michael, of the Order Elite, Class of the Hawk!"

Michael stepped forward and extended his hands. Carderas laid the spear across Michael's hands, and when he released it, Michael jerked slightly, his hands clamping down hard on the shaft of the spear. He bowed slightly to the commander over the spear, and blood welled between his fingers as he stepped backward to his place in the line. This process repeated for the other six—swords of varying size and shape for Kelvin, Sonia, Lyral, and Tarrason, a wickedly flanged mace for Kildare, and a morning star for Allan.

When it came to be Pelagir's turn, Carderas lifted forth a greatsword five feet long. He lifted it to the sky: "Sir Pelagir, of the Order Elite, Class of the Crown!" The others restrained themselves, but their surprise was obvious—Pelagir had become one of the King's Chosen, one of the king's bodyguards, spies, and assassins, ordinarily a slot reserved for a knight who had proven himself over years.

Pelagir bowed and took the hilt of his weapon, and pain entered him again. It was if thorns shot from the grip, sliding into his tendons and veins, and the blade hummed in his grasp. The red tint in the blade became more pronounced as the sword fed on Pelagir's blood and bound the two together. Even as Pelagir sheathed his weapon, he found that he understood its workings and its power, as if the knowledge had been implanted into his mind. And he realized that this blade was now his honor.

The Elite stepped back into formation. Carderas drew his sword and saluted the class with it, then swept the weapon toward the great gates. The Knights Assembled marched through them and into their new assignments.

That was the fourth graduation, and for a brief time, Pelagir felt united with his fellows.

On the side of the hill, just off the road, the lights of a tavern blazed into the early spring night. The dull murmur of a hard-working crowd crept through the open windows, and the child nestled in the crook of Pelagir's arm stirred restlessly. He guided his steed to a copse of trees nearby and dismounted. He watched the tavern for a few minutes, his eyes flickering from the windows to the doors, through which flowed a stream of customers. He loosened his sword in its scabbard, ran his fingers through his hair, and strode toward the tavern.

He pushed open the doors to a wash of noise and the smell of old beer and sawdust.

THE TAVERNER'S TALE

One account of Pelagir's encounters with civilization, as told by Kilroy, former proprietor of the Half-Eagle Tavern and Inn. Recorded by Winthorn, Knight of the Order Faithful, Class of the Rose, Rank Five.

You want to know about the man who burned my tavern? The man who destroyed my livelihood and left me homeless and begging? The man who stole my right hand from me and left me for dead? All right. I see the darkness in your eyes, like the kind he had, and I'm not fool enough to try to gull your kind twice.

'Twas a dark night, and the clouds were rollin' across the moon. The tavern was full that evening, the rough customers who make up most of my trade drinking and quarrelling and chatting up the ladies who use the upper rooms—and I don't know what their business is up there, lords, I just rent 'em the rooms—and it seemed like it was going to be just another busy night at the Half-Eagle Tavern. Figured that meant I was out at least a dozen mugs, two tables, five chairs, and three squares of tar paper in the window-holes. Good thing it was a busy night—it'd more than make up for the damage they'd be doing.

Of course, I'd be paying all the taxes on my take. Never missed a collection yet, sirs, so don't you be eyeing me up like that. I keep a good running tally in my head of what I make and what I spend. I've got a good memory.

Anyway, like I was saying, the night was shaping up to be a good one. It was windy enough that the nip was in the air and people'd want to be out of the cold, but not so cold that they'd want to stay in their drafty houses when I had a fire roaring. Perfect tavern night, in other words, and most of the drinking part of town was visiting. It was a good night for old feuds to flare up. Or for new feuds to come calling.

I recognized him for trouble the moment he walked in. No one in their right mind brings a baby into a roadhouse unless they're desperate and in need of something. The sorts of people who usually come into my place, well, they can smell that desperation. This is a hard-working town, lords, and the folks around here don't take well to strangers, and since no one saw him coming in, no one thought anything of it. Now, he was carrying a sword at his side and a knife at his other, but begging your pardon, being on the road to Terona we see plenty of fops who think a sword's for decoration, if you get my meaning. Besides, he was dirty and his clothes were rumpled and sweat-stained but obviously good quality. That made him a natural target. Likely on the run, not wanting to call official attention to himself, and probably with a fat purse for an enterprising lad.

Some of the local boys like to try these would-be nobles out. When their target's a dirty, tired-looking rich man carrying a baby, well, the pickings start to look a lot easier, if you catch my meaning. They don't kill the unlucky ones, but they do leave the travelers wishing they'd taken a different route.

I watched them size up the stranger out of the corners of their eyes, and I added a few more repairs to the carpenter's bill come morning. I ain't a hero, and I ain't going to stop 'em from a bit of fun.

He got himself a table by the fire, ordered some warmed milk for the little baby, who was starting to get a little cross, and some bread and meat for himself, with water to drink. That provoked a few sniggers from the boys at the nearby table, but they died quick enough to keep him from getting suspicious. I brought all this out to him.

It started innocently enough, but I knew what was happening. I kept looking up to see when it was going to start, see if I could guess what was coming next. I must have looked up four or more times between the intended victim and the thugs. These things develop a sort of pattern, you see, and it usually starts with a spilled drink, a couple of "accidental" shoves, and if the target don't take the bait, why, it just becomes a little more obvious. This man, I figured he'd be taking offense with the first or second spill, especially if it involved the baby.

I misread that night for sure. It took longer than usual to start, and that was a bad sign, because it meant the boys were working up for a serious beating. The drunker they got, the harder they hit and the later they stopped. I wanted to pass word to him that he was in for a bad night, and maybe to put the baby somewhere safe, but it wouldn't've been safe for me, and I had to live there... so I just let it go and kept my counsel to myself.

It took at least an hour. The man finished his food and tended to the child, and when they were both satisfied, the kid dozed off. He closed his eyes by the fire, too, leaning back against the wall, and it looked for all the world like he was sleeping.

That was pretty much the perfect moment for the boys to start in, and they took their best shot. A hell of a shot it was, too—a shout and hurled mug of beer started the whole mess off. The mug crashed into the wall by the man's head, too close to the baby for my comfort, and that's when the boys would have pretended to be fighting amongst themselves.

Only the man moved way too fast for them to even start their false fight. Much faster than that—faster than any man I've ever seen. Before the pieces of the mug hit the floor, before Big Tom was even done recovering from the throw, before the baby could even start crying under the wet of the beer, that man was off his bench with his naked blade in his hand. He skewered Big Tom right in the shoulder, ending Tom's throwing days for good, and then he slipped that big sword across Tom's throat, ending Tom's breathing and swallowing days for good, too.

Big Tom fell backward. His friends looked at the body.

The man looked at them. His sword arm hung loose and relaxed at his side, and his sword hummed just under hearing so you could feel the power in the thing. That's when we all knew him for one of the King's Chosen.

The boys looked at each other and then at the stranger. Their night got a whole lot more serious then, and I could see them calculating their odds: a good five to one, and likely the rest of the tavern'd be on the side of the local boys. But then, he was one of the fabled Knights of the Empire, and that meant blood. That meant they'd have to finish him, and do it before he got the law on them.

The locals watched the boys, then, ready to follow whatever card they played. With the eyes of the town on them, the boys didn't have much choice. Wordlessly they went for him. Their neighbors came in right after, bent on avenging Big Tom, and they meant to kill the man, never you mind that Tom started it or that they were against one of the King's Chosen.

Now, I help out during the Harvest Festival, and I've seen people reaping the wheat and barley, and sometimes someone drinks a little too much and starts spinning and cutting down the stalks without a care for how they fall. This man was like that. He ducked and spun and turned and everywhere he went his sword went, too, leaving stumps and blood spraying in its wake and the bodies of the townsfolk toppling. There wasn't a wasted movement that I could see. He made my customers look slow and stupid, and maybe they were, but he was so much faster than them that they never laid a hand on him, let alone one of their cudgels.

It was a massacre in there, the place laid to shambles. All I could do was stand behind the counter with my mouth open. I couldn't even run for help.

When he was finished with his work, there wasn't a single person moaning. They were all dead, and the blood was running in freshets from their wounds.

He sat down again, his bloody blade dripping on my table, and those dead eyes looked at me and nailed me to the spot. I ain't a coward, but I knew right then that he'd kill me if I gave him the slightest offense, and I went on my belly like a dog. I didn't care then if I disgusted him, and I don't care now. Way I figure it, if he felt contempt for me, he'd despise me, but he wouldn't want to put a sword in me, except maybe out of pity. And I thought that his sword had just tasted battle, and that he wouldn't want to execute someone after that heat. I guess I was right, too.

Anyway, he fixed me with his eyes, and in that monotone voice he started talking. Said something like, "This is a bad time, taverner. We've all turned into sheep, because we ain't got the sense to know who's a good ruler anymore. We just let those arselickers in Terona make our decisions for us, and it's making us animals, not people, and when we get too smart to keep our heads down, why, we ask for someone to put our eyes out so we don't see too close. And then those bastards in charge take our eyes like they're doing us a favor."

Now look, I don't agree with what he was saying. I'm telling you what he said.

So then he kept going, saying, "We don't believe in real heroes anymore. We believe in jesters and mummers and monsters who suck away our dreams and give their tiny visions, and instead of trying to dream bigger than that we pretend this is the limit of the world."

His voice held me there, and I knew he was speaking treason but I didn't have the strength to stop him. It seemed like he was speaking too much sense then. Not that I agree with it, though, oh no! He talked longer in that vein while the fire died down on the hearth behind him and the bodies started cooling, and I think he'd have kept talking 'til dawn came if the baby hadn't started crying then.

He let those eyes slip off me then to focus on the infant, and I found I could breathe again. He set the baby down on the bench gentle as can be, stood, turned from me, and stoked the fire 'til it burned brightly again.

"Pack me a bundle, taverner. Include bread, milk, water, and whatever fruits you have in season. Pack the best you have, if you value your life."

I hurried off to do that. I don't think there was any doubt in his mind that I'd follow his order. When I was done, I came back and laid the pack down beside his blade.

He didn't take his eyes off the child, but he grabbed my right wrist and pinned it to the table.

"Taverner." His eyes met mine.

"Yes, m'lord?" I tried to keep my voice from quaking.

"You knew what they were planning."

"No, my lord, no! I had no idea!"

"You lie, taverner. I saw you watching me. I saw you watching them. You thought of warning me, but instead held your tongue. You also overcharged me for the inferior food you brought before you knew who I might be.

You thought you'd take advantage of a tired man, a man who needed help."

"No, Sir Knight, no, that's not the case, no," and I found my tongue running away from me as he settled the baby down into his lap. I tried to tear my hand away, but his grip was like stone. He drew his knife from his belt, said, "You'll suffer only lightly for your sins," and took my hand off with a single blow.

He let go of my spouting wrist and picked up his sword as I howled. It hummed to life again, and I crawled backward away from him, and I knew then what my death looked like. But instead of killing me, he grabbed my stump and laid his blade on it and the blood stopped spraying from the wound, and that hurt worse'n all the rest put together.

He stood above me, and I could see he was tired, but oh lords, still powerful! I curled up on the floor. He wiped his blade on my shirt and stuck it back into its sheath. He turned and picked up the baby and bundle of food. He bent to the hearth and picked up a piece of burning wood and walked toward the door while I struggled to stand up. He stopped at the door and said, "Get out."

I hurried past him, and as I rushed out, he tossed the brand behind him into the tinder by the fireplace. Then he told me that I better not put it out, or I'd find out that losing my hand wouldn't be the worst thing that could happen to me.

He took himself to the trees right over there. I saw metal glimmering in the firelight from behind me, and it moved out of the woods and I realized it was his metal horse. He swung himself up and rode west without looking back as my inn burned.

I didn't dare put it out. The villagers who came to put out the flames stopped when they saw the bodies inside. Even those who might have helped, I stopped—I didn't want him to come back, because I know you fellows always keep your vows.

The village put me out because they thought I'd had something to do with the deaths of their friends, even when I showed them where I used to have a hand. I was lucky to escape town with my life.

I've been without a home ever since, begging because I have no hand and know no other work. He stole everything from me. The way I figure it, the knighthood owes me at least a way to get out of the fix I'm in.

And I been helpful to you, ain't I?

Recommendation: Execute this man for treason.
Recorded,

    Winthorn

RECOMMENDATION SIGNED

THE SAILOR'S TALE

The errant knight met me on the streets of Westport. He offered money—and steel to back it up—for us to carry him to his destination, but we turned him down. We thought that'd be the end of it.

The dockhands shouted curses at each other as they heaved the *Ocarina* to. We waited on board 'til they had finished, and when the massive breakwater gates slammed shut at the mouth of the harbor, we started off-loading our cargo. As usual, we were exchanging friendly insults and stories with the lubbers about the far-flung coasts we'd seen, but aside from the storms, the trip wasn't anything special, not like the time we'd seen a wizard's castoff eyeing the ship hungrily and we had to waste ten shots from the heavy guns at it. The ports we'd visited had been dull, deadly dull. So we invented some tall tales to make 'em feel like they were missing out on more than salt spray. But our hearts wasn't in it, and they could tell, too. They didn't rise to any of our half-hearted jokes, and that put a damper on *everyone's* night.

When it was done, we wanted to get to the Hulden guildhouse, get our pay, and go drinking—that might put some life back into us, but likely it'd take another sea voyage to wash this taste from our hearts. Besides, it was a dark night, and the sky was low with spring clouds, and none of us wanted to spend any more time in what would likely be a hell of a gusher when the clouds finally let loose. Still, we gathered the local gossip and discovered that we'd have the guildhouse to ourselves, a rare occurrence indeed—the other ships the Huldens or the Dengs controlled weren't due in for a few days or had left earlier in the afternoon, laden with parts from the forges, steamshops, and alchemical presses. There was a single dirigible docked at the mast in the square, and that meant no friendly rivalries with those crews. We could have passed our time by visiting the guildhouses of other merchants, but that usually led to brawls, and we'd have enough of those in the days ahead, we figured. That was a last-ditch effort for fun.

Loading done, we collected our pay chits from Galves, the first mate, gathered our gear, and tramped up the hills of Westport to our bunks at the Hulden Sailors Guild. If you've never been, it's a low-slung, rough stone building, with hewn beams and arches holding its weight. With some crowding, it can hold about three ships' worth of sailors—about three hundred. The ranking officers and mates stay on board their ship. The guild's outer walls are dark and its windows are small and high—after weeks or months on the high seas, most of us've had enough of the damned sun.

Well, except for sailors like me. My name's Camila Voris. I'm a tiller's engineer, so I spend most of my time below decks, slaving away on the great gears that keep the boat moving in the direction Captain "Early" Jon Meyels wants it to go. Working sixteen-hour shifts don't give me much latitude to get up on deck, and when I do, I haven't usually got time to watch the scenery, but what I do see, I hold as close to my heart as my lungs. I take the best chance I can to make up for that lost freedom when we hit land and we're laid over for two weeks. So naturally, the weather set me off—I'd been hoping for sun and shine, and instead I got this coming rain. My berthmates, Pol Austin and Skag Madison, recognized it in me and kept mum, or more likely were as glum at the thought of rain. Even if we're not aching for the sight of sun on land, none of us fancies being trapped inside during our leaves.

So that might explain why we were less than courtly polite when we found our way blocked by that young man.

Let me tell you about the *Ocarina*. She's a fast vessel—not one of the fastest, but fast. She's tough, too—again, not the toughest, but tough. She's outrun the pirates of Elsidon and gunned down their fastest scout when it wouldn't give up the pursuit. She's a cutter with a steam engine that provides us enough power to haul heavy cargoes or other vessels and still make it to our destination on time, or else to put on a burst of speed when we're running high. She's got three heavy guns and two light guns each to port and starboard, and the ironclad hull boasts a tempered-steel prow in case someone gets a little too friendly with us. She's got three masts on the deck and three levels below-decks, and one of those masts can double as a mooring for a light dirigible if we've got our heavy anchors down. The steerhouse sits on the top of two levels at the stern of the ship, with mage-hardened windows all 'round. She's got a speaking-tube system that lets the captain communicate across the ship, and he runs the ship hard and well. He runs the ship for House Hulden, and they lease her services to other merchant Houses of the Empire, at least in name. In practice, Early Jon picks and chooses the contracts he wants, and he's good enough and generous enough that he's kept his sailing crew working with him for years. He's canny in the ways of the sea, he rises before us and is abed after. The *Ocarina* is the best ship most of us've ever sailed on, and it's because of that that we're in the position we're in today.

"Out of the way," Pol snarled, and she reached out to shove the interloper aside. I say she *reached* because he wasn't there when her hand got to where he'd been.

"Don't do that," the stranger said. His voice was flat, his face empty, and it nailed Pol to the spot. If he'd flashed or growled, she might have tried again. She backed down, though, the first time I'd ever seen her do that. And now, thinking back on it, I think she might be a better fighter than I ever thought, because I guess she never got into a fight she wasn't sure she could win, and she never'd backed down before. At least not in front of me. But this time, she put her hands down and spoke.

"What do you want?"

"I need to speak to your captain," the stranger said. "I need a ship, a fast one, for myself, my charge, and my steed."

"Guild's empty," I said. "We're just in, and we ain't leaving."

"You will. I can pay."

Skag broke in: "We won't. We been out to sea for a month now, and we're due leave. You won't find a crew willing to take you for at least a few days, unless you have truly excellent money." Skag looked the man up and down. "A lot more than it looks like you're carrying." Skag had been third mate before he'd been busted back down, and he knew how a ship ran. "Anyway, the captain won't see anyone 'til he's seen to the replenishing of the ship."

"I do not ask," the man said. "I require." His hand drifted to his sword handle, idly, slowly, and it was suddenly perfectly clear to me that it wasn't idle at all, that this man didn't make threats, not like sailors do.

"But you *can't* require," continued Skag. "Our ship is light-staffed as it is, and our sailors have spread through the city. No way we can run a ship without our men, and no way we'll be able to find them all in this city in the next few days. They're at the whorehouses or the gambling dens, or they've headed out into the country. Like I said, we're due leave, and our sailors take it when they get it. They'll hear if we put the word out that there's more money to be made, but I don't make any guarantees."

The stranger looked at us, one after the other, studying us. Though he didn't like it, he saw the truth in our faces like sun off the water. He nodded, tilted his head a tiny piece, and said, "My apologies for the waste of your time. I shall return tomorrow evening to speak with your captain, and with enough money to hire your services." He turned and headed up toward Candlemaker's Square. That's when the clouds broke, and that's when we bolted in.

We spent that night inside, playing cards and drinking ale, cursing the weather. It poured through the night, filling the hilly streets of Westport with the water the clouds'd reclaimed from the sea. When we stepped out the next morning, I was surprised there weren't fish flopping in the gutters and dying on the stones. The alchemical smears from the presses had been washed away, down to harbor, leaving the streets momentarily bright and clean. The day was dry, though the sky promised to unload some more water on us later. It was under that sky that our first full day of leave began.

What does a sailor do on leave? What do we do when we're off that boat after a month or more cooped up together?

That's an answer I'll leave to your imagination, but I can guarantee that most of us spent the day in the seedier parts of town, the kinds of places with proprietors who give their cut to the Bhumar thugs who stand quietly in the corners. And despite having seen the same faces in close quarters for all that time, I can guarantee that most of us spend our leave in the company of our shipmates—from what I hear, it's like how small-town folks never move away for fear of the strange, how they stay and marry the same people they've seen all their lives and never cut the apron strings that hold 'em close to home. In our case, though, it's different. Every day we're someplace else, every day we're cast on the waves.

But even sailors need someplace to call home. Our shipmates are our anchors, the islands in the sea of time. So we find our homes in them.

We spent the day doing those things that make vice lords richer and us poorer, and who's to say who came out of it better? Of course, we split off from each other at one point or another and took care of our own business. Me, I went looking for the scenery and for new people to talk to. Over by the steamworks, I found a pilot who called himself Dracogen, who flew in the Deng fleet, but he'd got himself drunk and they lifted off without him, so here he was, stranded and without a paycheck, and would I be so kind as to lend him a coin or two. Seeing as he'd worn out his welcome with the pressers, I took him with me back to our part of town and introduced him around. Some of our crew'd been drifters once, and they put him to the test. Maybe he was what he said or maybe he was playing a beautiful con, but either way, he'd keep us entertained enough that he'd be guaranteed to drink and whore for free for days. He was pretty enough that he wouldn't have trouble on that end, that's for sure.

I left him with the crew and headed back to the guildhouse around the afternoon—they don't stock many male whores in that town, and I don't much care for the other kind. I'm a terrible gambler, and I'd had enough of walking the streets through the stink of the foundries, commercial and naval, and besides, the sky was filling the morning's promise: I saw another fall storm coming in over the horizon to the west, and I didn't want to be caught in any part of it. I came back to rest my feet, read the sheets, and relax a bit in the quiet. I tossed a nod to old Kip the doorman and headed back to my alcove. I drew the curtains around me, and sleep was on me before I knew it.

The rest of the crew started spilling in after night fell, some of 'em for a change of clothes and others to sleep off whatever drunk they'd started earlier in the day. I woke to their cursing, their laughter, their muttering about the storm that'd broken outside. I lay in bed with my solitude, close enough to their warmth.

I heard the wind howl as the front door opened, the spatter of rain on the tiles inside, and my mates' shouts to heave the door—and then I heard those shouts die in their throats. I heard feet beating war and death on the floor, and I planted an eye on the gap between my curtains.

This is what I saw:

Four knights—not the ordinary kind, these; they were at least a step up from infantry in the army. These were stronger, surer, even inside the steel armor that covered them. Two men, two women, smooth faces, and the eyes of killers. They wore the bars of the king on their shoulders, and their armor moved with every motion they made. Didn't betray a sound. Their hands rested on the hilts of their sheathed swords. Two of them stood by the front door, and the other two stepped to the center of the room. The woman stood with her back to me and spoke, her voice icy as the northern waters.

"I am Captain Alna Drake, a Knight of the Order Faithful, Class of the Shield, Rank Two. I am here on a mission from the Crown, and you are all hereby ordered to submit to my pleasure and my will. Do any of you object?" She paused for a second or two. "I take silence as assent."

We were all mute.

"A man came to this building yesterday, shortly after you finished unloading your vessel. He was a young man, about twenty-one years of age. He was armed with a sword. He was young, dark of hair and lean of build. He was likely carrying a baby girl with him as well. We believe he was seeking passage. He stood here and left just before the storm broke. We believe he spoke to some of you. If any of this is untrue, speak now."

Again, silence.

"I ask again, are there any variances in my suppositions? Are there any details I have missed?"

I was watching Pol and Skag, so I saw Pol swallow before she stepped forward. "He didn't have the baby."

"You spoke with him yourself?"

"Aye—I mean, yes."

"Was anyone else present?"

Pol said, "No," but her eyes must've flicked to Skag. The knight near the captain stepped forth briskly and took Skag's arm and dragged him out of line. I thanked the gods that I was still in my bed, because it might have been me that Pol shot that glance to.

"No," Pol protested. She looked like she wanted to sit down, and I could feel the blood draining from my face. I could smell violence coming.

"I said I require cooperation, and I mean to get it. You, man, you were with her?"

". . . Yes," said Skag. His face was white and he was shaking.

"You did not respond to my earlier questions. You did hear me when I outlined the details, correct?"

"Yes."

"And you heard me declare my right to detain you all for questioning?"

"Yes."

"Then I accuse you of hindering an Imperial investigation. Do I have a witness to this crime?"

The knight holding Skag's arm spoke, his voice gravel. "I witnessed this crime."

"Then by the power invested in me by the king, and by the Count of Westport, and by the magistrates and the laws thereunto, I sentence this man— what's your name, sailor?"

"Skag Madison." He'd have collapsed to the floor if the knight hadn't been holding him.

"Then, Skag Madison, for your crime, I hereby sentence you to execution, such sentence to be carried out immediately. Vastone, you are executioner tonight."

"Yes, m'lady," said Skag's captor—Vastone—and he snapped Skag's arm with a twist of his hand. Skag dropped to his knees with a cry of pain, and even as he was falling, Vastone's hand was on the hilt of his sword. Before Skag hit the ground, the sword was out. And while Skag was screaming, Vastone took his head clean off.

The *Ocarina's* sailors began to step forward and were met with the quick-drawn swords of the other knights—the two at the door had left their posts during Skag's mock of a trial. Somehow, these four seemed as though they'd be more than capable of taking a crew of a hundred. Worse, they didn't seem especially worried about the fight, and that's what kept the crew from rushing 'em.

Drake said, "Do not compound his error. You and you," she pointed with her sword, "get this body out of here. The rest of you—"

"Should do nothing. I have words for these four, and they should be shared." Our stranger had entered quietly, and now he stood just inside the door, his arms crossed. I got up from my bed so I could better see what was happening.

The Knights Faithful immediately moved into a crescent around him, and I realized that these four, who had shown no thought toward fighting an entire shipload of sailors, were wary of this one man, like they thought he might outmatch them.

The captain broke the awful silence first. "Pelagir." Her voice was just so slightly shaking.

"Captain Drake," he replied. "I admit surprise that you found me so soon. I thought I traveled quickly and quietly enough." His eyes flicked to the two who had been guarding the door, to the one at the captain's side, and he gave them a nod. "Givens. Teroux. Vastone." His attention turned back to the captain.

"It was not your stealth that betrayed you, Sir Pelagir. Blame your blade, and blame your courser. Blame your excruciation. When your devices were bound to you, the Archmagus worked his will on them. They speak to him from afar, and to those who carry his devices. Even now, reinforcements are coming here, seeking you. Therefore, Sir Pelagir Amons, son of Sir Pelgram Amons, you are under arrest for high crimes against the Empire, and you are commanded to place yourself under our power."

As she spoke, Pelagir stepped slowly toward the center of the room, his hands dropping to his sides, and the other knights closed the circle around him. Their blades were still in their hands, pointed directly at the man. He did not draw the sword at his side. Instead, he bowed to the captain, a curious bow that put one foot in front of the other and twisted his body so that his arms crossed his body front and back, right in front and left behind.

His eyes, his cold eyes, were on her alone: "My lady, I invite you to test your power, and to see if it can hold me before your reinforcements arrive."

The five exploded into action. Never have I seen such a display of combat, and likely never will again. As the four lunged at him, he leapt from the ground, and his hands and feet struck the four blades—*each on the flat*— knocking them wildly astray. Givens and Teroux nearly impaled each other, and Drake and Vastone crossed swords before checking their attack. Pelagir landed on two hands and a knee, his right leg extending out behind him. His eyes raked Drake and Vastone, judged them pacified for the moment, and he swept his right leg under Teroux's feet as he pivoted and took his own feet, and Teroux toppled to the floor. One quick stride, and he was stamping on the man's throat with his left foot and deflecting a furious attack by Givens with his bare hands. As the downed one began to color and strangle, Pelagir feinted with his left hand, drew another short chopping attack from Givens, and grabbed the man's sword hand. Drake and Vastone advanced on him, and Pelagir threw Givens at them—lifted him off the ground and tossed him, armor and all.

Drake sidestepped the flying body, but Vastone took him full force. The two went down in a clatter. And while they fought to regain their feet, Pelagir fought this captain of the Knights Faithful with his bare hands, spinning, ducking, deflecting. As the other two knights stood and rushed, Pelagir stepped in close to her and slapped her twice, lightly, scornfully. He leapt back behind the body of the fallen knight, who was choking out his last breaths, and for the first time, a smile came to his lips. Three Knights Faithful facing him, side by side, with naked blades, and he smiled.

"Do you yield?" he asked. Drake licked her lips and looked at the other two. As she calculated the possibilities, Pelagir slowly drew his own blade, and we all knew it for a blade of power. "Of course not. You are Faithful. Your loyalty is well known." It seemed like he was making a joke, but it was so hard to tell. He sketched a salute. "Farewell."

We all knew then that it is true what they say: the Archmagus makes knights who are not human. I could not follow all his movements, and though the three Knights Faithful were skilled warriors, among the best living in the Empire, they were only human. They couldn't hope to best this cyclone.

One by one, and quickly, they fell. Drake was last. She got beaten to her knees, and Pelagir beheaded her before she could beg for mercy. I suppose that's what's considered "guarding your honor" among the knights. Sailors call it killing.

He stood there among all the bodies, and then he said to us, "Sailors, you are outlaws now. Had you left before you saw me, your lives would be safe. But now you are as complicit in my crimes as I. You heard the captain before she died—reinforcements are coming, and they will surely sweep you under their feet. I suggest you pack your gear, take whatever supplies you need from this guild, and move quickly down to the wharf. I have spoken to... to Early Jon. Your ship will sail in two hours, and you had best be on it if you wish to escape the wrath of the Empire.
Tell no one of what you have seen here tonight, unless you wish them to be hunted, tortured, and executed, as befalls traitors to the Empire's glory."

He drove his sword into the floor and left. Its handle was thorn-strewn and dripped with blood. It hummed for a moment and died as the door closed behind him.

Silence followed him out the door, and the place exploded with talk and shouts.

"Leave? But we just got here!"

"No way I'm following him. No way."

"But what about the Empire?"

"Are we supposed to be pirates now? I don't hold with piratin', but I ain't no landlubber, and I can't give up the sea."

"What are you going to do? Try to explain to the constables—hell, the damn *army*!—why we're standing around the corpses of four knights?"

"Why can't we hide the bodies, deny they were ever here?"

"You think you'd hold up under torture? I don't know that I'd trust any of you not to break! I wouldn't trust myself!"

All the while, I was packing my gear quietly. When I finished, I shouted to make myself heard over the babble. When everyone quieted down, I said, "There's one good reason we have to leave now."

"What's that?" someone asked.

"Remember how the captain said they found him?" I pointed to the sword Pelagir'd left on the floor. "They know he was here. They think he's *still* here. And all the time you're standing around talking about it and not packing your gear, they're getting ready to mount a raid in here that'll be able to take that man down. You think we'd be able to fight against that? No way. I'm a sailor on the *Ocarina*, and a sailor I'm gonna stay. We've got no other ships to run to, we don't know our way around the land, and they'll crush us if they catch us here. Best bet for you is to get on the *Ocarina*, get to another port, and sign on to another vessel. I'm going to stick with the vessel I love, if Early Jon'll have me after we're done with this. But one way or another, I'm leaving this place and these bodies, and I tell you that you'd best get out of here before they come."

I shouldered my bag and walked toward the door. Pol did the same, and we strode down the hill to the waiting ship together. It was all we could do to keep from running, but we didn't want to draw attention.

I'd like to say that it was a mad dash out the harbor, that the army chased us down the hill, that the rusty gates of the breakwater scraped the metal off the stern, and that we fought off two of the Imperial Navy's fastest clippers. But it wasn't like that, not at all. All our sailors made it down the *Ocarina* right smart, and Galves and Early Jon had always been sharp about immediate provisioning. Pol went up to tell him about Skag and what happened in the guildhouse. She'd barely finished when Pelagir loped up the gangway, carrying himself a new sword—a big, nasty piece of work, slung over his back—and a baby in his arms. She was looking around as alert as any seaman in a crow's nest, and she was quiet, too. He spotted me before I headed below-decks, and summoned me to him.

"Has the captain made the necessary preparations? Is the ship ready for traveling?"

"Aye, she is, but you'll need to speak to the captain to tell him what happened. He's up in the steerhouse. Pol Austin's just told him the score, but he's going to want to hear it from you—I hope you're worth all this trouble."

"I spoke with him already, and he knows my worth, sailor. I would have words with you when I have finished with him."

"Good enough."

He took off to the 'house, and I followed behind him—but slow, meandering. I didn't get to hear much of what they said, but it sounded like Pelagir was warning the captain of what'd happen to those of us who'd been in the guildhouse, something about the Empire falling, and something about the child. Something about insurance.

Even as he spoke, Captain Meyels got us moving right quick, and I suppose he got the harbormaster to open the gates for us under one lie or another. Whatever the truth, we hit the open sea far faster than we'd had any reason to believe we would. We all tasted relief as the land disappeared behind us.

Once we were out of sight of land, Pelagir sought out Early Jon again. I was out on the deck, helping secure this and that, and putting off going into the tiller-chamber as long as possible. When he left the steerhouse, the ship headed sharp south, and Pelagir moved port to watch the dark clouds over the land. His sea-legs were impressive, though I suppose it could have been expected. I walked over to join him.

We stood at the rail as the shoreline receded in the distance. He held the child in his left arm, cradled against his body, and she watched the waves glide past us with uncommon interest. Quiet, for a few minutes.

"Where've you been keeping the kid?" I asked.

"In a safe place, with trusted companions I met in the wars," he replied, not meeting my eyes. "I will not endanger them by saying more."

"Who is she?"

"I am sure you will find out soon enough. Let us call her protection against the darkness that rises from our Empire's old heart."

"So you're not going to tell me, then? Not after you've made us all outlaws and pirates?"

He watched me out of the corner of his eye, saw me watching him, and raised an eyebrow. "Have you sworn any oaths, sailor?"

"You mean promises or curses? I've had a couple either way."

"Is there anything so pure to you that you would die sooner than see it violated?"

"Nothing comes immediately to mind, but I'm sure I could... well, freedom, I suppose. The freedom of the open seas, of fast currents and the deep. You took that away from me, I don't know what I'd do."

"Then I ask that you hold this in confidence sacred to that freedom. I have devoted my life to the service of the Empire. I have given over my humanity that I might protect it better. I have killed and nearly been killed so that it could stand for another day, another year."

"I've heard tell of the knights and their oaths, sure."

"It is more than an oath for us. It is our life's blood. It is our reason for breathing." He paused to shift the child. "This is a prelude to answering your question."

"All right."

"What do you do when your existence proves to be false? When you discover that a cancer gnaws at the very heart of your belief? Do you cut it away although it sits at the heart, and hope that the wound is not fatal? Or do you seek other remedies that might have a chance of success?"

"I'd say cutting out from the heart would be a last resort."

"As would I. Certain things were told to me, truths that opened my eyes. My unbreakable vow began to crack, and it shattered when I realized our king was a dotard, and that the foundation on which the Empire was built so long ago was beginning to shift and erode away. A man came to me then, and told me how it could be saved—for the good of all, he said, so that none would have to face the chaos that ruled before King Martyn. Because of my love for the Empire, I betrayed my oath and helped lay the plans that would overthrow the king. But I soon began to see that this new warlord thought not of the Empire, but only of enriching himself, and his friends as well. They gathered darkness to themselves, and with darkness they deceived many. I among them. I had seen what I wanted to see, and it was only through accident that I discovered their true nature. With one stroke my part in their plot became clear."

"But what does this have to do with the girl?"

"The trap was to have been sprung on the equinox. We had slowly gathered allies across the reaches of government, telling them the king would be put to exile. Instead, the traitors would assassinate the king and his family, and the conspirators would take their place. I was to have been one of these assassins."

"But?" I asked.

"But I arrived early to a meeting, and I heard the man who claimed to be my friend tell his companion what was to become of the assassins. 'Broken toys,' he said, 'tools now useless. Once they have betrayed one oath, the rest of the betrayals will come more quickly. We will arrange for them to be seen, if possible captured and executed, and thus expose the rest of the knighthood as corrupt. If they cannot be captured, why, that will be proof that the knighthood is not willing to provide justice to its own.' I left silently and returned at the appointed time. They acted as ever and gave me no clue that they were planning to betray not only me, but the knighthood as well."

"What did you do?"

"On the night that we were to spring the trap, I traveled to the nursery and..." He swallowed here, remembering. "I went to the nursery where the king's daughters slept, and took what child I could. I could save only one before the reinforcements came. I took my courser and sped west. This is Caitrona, the only surviving member of that family. I take her to safety and will act as her guardian until such time as she is ready to assume the throne."

"Are you saying that the king is dead?"

"He must be. Those who slew him are already taking power. I could not warn the other members of my order; I had already betrayed them in my heart and in deed, in carrying details of the Council of Knights to Athedon. Forsworn as I was, my words would have been seen as more treachery. Instead of acting, I tried to think my way through the plot, and instead of telling my brothers, I chose to wait and see how things would unfold. At the end, when it was far too late, I raised my voice to my captain, and when he commanded me slain, I discovered that he too had been forsworn. As for the rest of my order, I can only hope that they escape before the conspirators' trap closes on them."

"What if the princess doesn't want to rule? What if the new king proves to be a better ruler than the last one?" I could barely think of the questions—too much was coming at me, too fast.

"She will be taught of duty, honor, and necessity. As for the new ruler . . . I cannot say. The Birdsnest Wars brought us King Fannon, and this coup seemed likely to be less bloody in the short term, and that was my focus when I joined them." He struck himself in the leg, reprovingly. "Fool that I was! Yet I think it unlikely that Athedon's policies will benefit the Empire greatly. Looking back now, I think he sought power for power, not for duty. His hunger for power will weigh too greatly on the wheel of the state, and he will veer too far to protect himself. His policy of distrust has already caused one defection, at least—who knows how many more will flee once he has entrenched himself?

"Regardless," he continued, "their strength has grown too great for me to fight alone. Better to retreat now and return when the time is right, when they have driven the populace into terror. I believe the old way to have been strict but just, and—"

I scoffed. "Just? You think the Empire is just? Friend, you've got a lot to learn. Now that you're out of Terona, maybe you'll see how *just* the Empire is on your own."

"I do not believe I will have that opportunity. I intend to disappear entirely."

"I don't suppose you're going to tell me where."

A faint smile appeared on his lips as answer.

"I'd bet I'm one of the few alive who knows even this much. If my life weren't forfeit before . . . I don't dare set foot in the Empire under my own name again, do I? You've taken all that away." A sadness began to well up in me, but I'd be damned if I'd let him see my tears. Besides, it was mixed with more than a share of a rage that would do me no good to show. "My shift is starting, Sir Knight, and I'd suggest you get below-decks as well. There's a storm coming from the west." I turned and left the rail. And then I stopped and turned, and spat, "I want to wish you the best of luck, but I want you to remember that you have destroyed all our lives. We're not just pieces in a game. Believe it or not, the subjects of the Empire have dreams, too. It's not all bowing to our betters and looking for ways to make their lives easier. Damn you, we just want to be left alone! Why in Hell would you do this to us?"

He had the grace to look abashed, and he said, "You have my apologies, sailor. I have been unfair. I only wanted my tale to be told. I wanted the truth spread before my reputation in history is slandered. I wanted... I wanted someone to absolve me."

"Then look to an ecclesiast," I said. "What I am is a sailor."

"But have I done the right thing?" he asked, almost plaintive, and I saw then the youth in his face, and I knew that he'd been pushed for too long, without a chance to be himself, and I was momentarily ashamed. But that vanished like a spray of mist against a sail: like it or not, we had taken a side.

"I don't know, Pelagir," I said. "What I know is that you've done it. Now you've got to see it through. It's you against the Empire now. You and the princess. Make sure you've got the right allies on your side." On impulse, I bowed to the girl. "And you, your Majesty, when you take your throne, let it be said that Camila Voris was the first to bow to you." I glanced at Pelagir, and said, "Remember that your subjects have lives of their own and minds of their own. May fair winds bless you all your life."

He frowned, his brows knitting in thought. "You have my thanks, and her thanks as well. Be well, Camila Voris, and hold your freedom dear."

I nodded curtly, descended to the tiller, and didn't see them again.

About two hours later, we took the ship hard to port and set the engines to idle for a time. Long enough for a skiff to set to shore and get back to the ship. That's the story and the truth. They told me he was heading inland, baby on his shoulder, his sword on his back.

But now I hear that the captain is going to tell us what's to become of us. I don't know what it is, but in my deepest heart, I hope that he won't tell us to abandon the *Ocarina*. I'll fight against the Navy if I have to, and I'll die if I must. This is the life I've chosen, and it's the life I mean to live.

THE SHEPHERD'S TALE

Winter, CY 585

The old man came out of the east as winter tightened its grip on the land. He crossed into my home pasture from the thin trees on the hill line on the heels of the dawn, and my two dogs, Inger and Crosh, started to barking soon as they saw him. There I was with my hand on the door to the pen and the sheep ready to move to the day's pasturage, and now comes a stranger to contend with. Well, I figured, the day's work can't be kept because of something different, unless it's a surprise that keeps the work from being done. I didn't see any wolves or fire, nor any poachers chasing the man, so I whistled up the dogs and opened the gate, and the boys got the sheep moving off into the western pasture I leased from the mayor of Dunlop, and I followed along slow so as to cross the old man's path. While I walked, I watched him and I kept a firm hand on my staff. I kept some surprises there.

Old he looked, my age. I'd've pegged him at sixty-five, seventy years. Shortish hair, looked like he'd cut it himself with a knife by a stream for the past few months. He'd let his beard grow out, which was a good thing, considering the cold the winter'd brought this year. Wasn't tall, neither, but he had that air of command you find in a few town councilmen or maybe old soldiers that made him seem taller. He was tired, too, like he'd been walking all night, and he looked like he'd walk another night if he needed to, but he didn't lean on his walking stick. When our paths grew near to crossing, I called to him.

"Morning, stranger."

"And to you, shepherd. My name is Toren. May I walk with you?"

"Can't stop you, I figure. Name's Ysabel."

"It's either a girl's name or you're from Amchester," he said.

"Right you are," I replied. "I left there shortly after the Siullan Uprising. Seemed like a better idea than being drafted."

"I fought in that war. Those were some hard times." He fell into step beside me. "How fare the sheep this winter?"

"Good. Had a few lost to wolves, a few fell sick, but mostly they thrive."

"Do you have need for another hand to help with the flock?"

I stopped to think about it, and he said quickly, "You need not worry about housing or feeding me. I can build my own shelter and hunt for or purchase my own food. I know how to live off the land, and I have money to pay for what I cannot forage."

"Then why ask to help at all?"

"Because I want to be useful to someone. I've spent my life being useful and active, and now that I'm done with my old life, I want to start a new one."

"A new life? Only people I knew who needed new lives were..." I looked at him keen and said, "Is the law after you? I won't hide a criminal."

"I am no criminal, friend. I'm just an old soldier looking for a new life."

He wasn't lying about that, but it wasn't the whole truth, as I found out later. He brought trouble to Dunlop, and a whole lot more, and quicker than we'd sought it.

He was as good as his word, at least as far as the work went. He caught on to the life of a shepherd quickly, and he kept to himself, mostly. I watched him for a time to be sure he wasn't going to steal away with my flock, but he showed no signs of it, and so I let my guard down.

Shepherding's solitary work, you know. After I'd taught him the commands for the dogs, shown him where the sheep ate best and where Lord Farthington's property line began to the east and the north, and the mayor's line to the west and south, it was about all he needed to know. I passed on more of the details to him on the nights we drank before the fire in my hut. I told him of the land, weather patterns, wolf signs and other dangers, the mating of the sheep, and the tasks we'd need to get done the next day—all the knowledge I'd picked up over the years since I'd come here, using the mind that I'd trained so early. Sometimes we talked about the wars he'd been in and the battles he'd fought, but he didn't seem to like talking about that much. He said that if I hadn't been in one, I wouldn't understand. Fair enough, I said, and poured more wine, and I held my tongue about my own past. Just as well, I suppose—no one likes to hear about failure.

After only a week, we fell into a routine. We'd meet in the morning to take the sheep out to pasture in the rocky hills, up where I'd leased some winter storage sheds for the sheep's forage. I'd have gotten the sheds closer, but one of them was conveniently near a hidden cave, and I'd set up some apparatus there, and having the sheep nearby gave me a good excuse to check in on it. I didn't want it too closely tied to me: the lawmen might consider it magic, and the Council of Magi might have some stern questions about it. I had enough of my tinkering lying around in my cupboards that I was already uncomfortable with having in the house, and I made an effort to get the worst of it away from prying eyes.

Besides, the land near my cottage was tied up in boundary disputes between Lord Farthington and the mayor of Dunlop—the usual tumult between two men of power who didn't care about the people who had to live with the consequences of their petty disagreements. I had no choice but to walk the flock or sell all the sheep. My situation wasn't rare in these parts, but we all got used to going out of our way. Can't say as we liked it, though. In fact, there were some of us who disliked it enough that... no, I'll save that for later.

We'd part at the fork that split the path around the central hill. From there, I took my herd to the eastern hill, and he took his to the slopes of Eagle Rock, the first mountain to the west, the flagship on the range that rode to the north and south ten miles off, the land between dominated by hills that broke more harshly as they neared the mountains. Our vale was the last usable land before the mountains, and though it was green enough, it was far too rough for cultivation. My sheep were of the Merck line, practically half goat anyway, so they could handle the uneven ground better than most of their kind. I got to practice my skills in my hidden cave, building more surprises like those of my shepherd's crook. Had any wolves or poachers—or lone lawmen—come across me there, they would scarcely have known how they died.

To the east, an offshoot of the Imperial coach road connected Dunlop—the largest town in the area, three miles to the south—to the rest of the world. Toren withdrew from sight when he spied travelers on the road. He watched the carriages thunder past on the main road to town and asked me about them when we met in the evening on the way back to the night pasture. A rare day it was that any of them had news, and when the news came, it came fast and dangerous as wolves in the mist.

Once a week, I headed into the village to help teach the children to read and write. It wasn't much, but they were eager for whatever scraps of knowledge came their way. There were a few others in town who were educated, and one or two who deigned to share that learning. The few books in town were worth more than gold to these children and their parents, and they guarded them against fires and brigands and grasping mayors alike.

But the cold winter had its own special dangers.

In the heart of winter, a bitter storm blew down from the north, strong enough that it seemed it had brewed up to cool the heels of the devilish hordes themselves. We had precious little warning that the season had this storm in store for us—the endless gray skies of winter gave no clue until the clouds lowered themselves down Eagle Rock. I drove my flock home as quick as I could, praying that Toren had read the signs aright, and cursing with what was left of my breath when I saw he hadn't. Fifteen shivering minutes it took me to lock the sheep in the winter barn, and the snow was falling heavy by the time I was done. It took another fifteen to hobble my way to the fork. By the time I reached it, the snow was coming down thick and white as ewe's wool, there was a good inch of fresh snow on the ground, and the wind was starting to howl. It was the worst storm I'd seen in years.

I met Toren at the fork, and he looked half wild.

"I've lost two!" he shouted at me over the wind, his teeth chattering his words short.

"Forget them!" I shouted back. "We'll never find them in this weather!"

We drove the rest of the flock back to the barn, no conversation coming between us, snatched away by the wind. When we reached the barn, Toren said, "You can't afford to lose those sheep, can you?" He knew the answer—I was barely scraping by. He said, "I'm going back after them."

"You idiot, those sheep are good as dead. You'll be dead, too, if you go after them."

"They're my responsibility. I lost them, and I will bring them back." He whistled up Inger and was gone, out the door into the howling storm. I cursed him as he left, but I had to let him go. I had to pen the sheep, and that took me a good five minutes. I followed him off as quick as I could, but he had more than enough of a head start.

I snatched my lantern and my crook and shivered my way into the storm after him, slogging through the bluster and the ice that drove into face and beard. The storm was thick enough that I nearly lost my bearings a couple of times—me, who'd spent the last twenty years on this land and knew every hillside like a brother—and had I the breath, I'd have heaved a sigh of relief when I reached the boulder that marked the fork in the road. Snow was covering Toren's footsteps even then, but I followed them into the dark and into the west.

All the landmarks were strange to me then, with the scrawny trees hanging their boughs under ice and a heavy load of snow. My only guides were the filling footsteps and, I hoped, the knowledge of the land I'd lived on for two decades. Up I struggled, my breath coming hard in my lungs and Crosh breasting the drifts by my side. The tracks I followed got shallower and shallower... I was falling behind and couldn't move any faster, and worse, if I recognized the trail here aright, Toren and the sheep were heading toward the rocky ravines on Eagle Rock. They'd be lucky to escape death this night. Hells, *I'd* be lucky to make it home to my bed, and I wondered why I kept on. Wasn't because he was the best friend I'd ever had, and he hadn't been around long enough for me to know what sort of man he was, if he was the sort of man worth sacrificing yourself for.

But I guess he was, because there I was doing it without thinking about it, and I supposed that meant that he had some effect on me. Not friendship, but... respect? But I couldn't spend my energy thinking. I had to fight the cold, watch the landmarks, listen for Toren and Inger and the sheep, keep moving, keep moving. The snow was deeper now, my breath coming hot and hard even as my toes numbed and my fingers hardened into claws. I was a fool for coming this far. I was a fool for coming out at all. I should have let him die in this frigid blast, I was only coming out because he'd taken my best dog with him, and I was going to turn around right... wait... was that... it was!

At the dead tree that marked the beginning of the truly treacherous ground, near the steep ravine, Crosh bounded forward barking at some dim shape in the snow. It was Toren, and he was holding Inger's hind legs over the mouth of the abyss, keeping the dog from plunging to his death, and his own feet were slipping toward that fall. I rushed for them as well as I could, kicking through the snow, and stepped sideways on a loose rock. It shot out from under my foot, and I slipped sideways and my foot landed in a small gulley. I heard my ankle snap, and I had a brief moment of dreadful clarity before agony took my sight. I fell forward on my face, and I flung my staff out to Toren, holding an end so that he could grab the other. He chanced a grab at it with his right hand, and at that moment his left hand slipped, and Inger slipped into the darkness, yelping like the puppy he had been years ago.

Somehow I held onto the staff long enough for Toren to grab hold of Crosh—who had run to his side—regain his balance, and pull himself back from the precipice. He rushed to me, and pulled me up from the ground. I blanked momentarily as my bones ground against each other, and came to with my arm around his shoulder, being dragged down the mountain. "Come on, Crosh, lead us home," he was urging the dog, and Crosh led us unerringly down the hillside. We fought the wind and snow the whole way down, trusting in our faithful guide to bring us to safety and warmth—two old men, one lame, herded by a sheepdog through a howling storm.

By all rights, we should have been dead, and I fell in and out of wakefulness. I had no choice. I pressed a stud on my crook, and its head blazed into fire. Toren recoiled from me, and I'd have fallen if not for the staff.

"There's a cave near here," I croaked, gesturing. "We need to get there.

Can't... can't make it in this snow. Crosh, *avantis*." My faithful dog altered his course, and Toren made up his mind. He caught my arm, draped it over my shoulder, and carried the blazing staff before us to my hidden shelter.

The last thing I remember of that night is Crosh's whine, his teeth on my sleeve as he pulled on me, the snow driving into my face, hissing in the staff's blaze, and the realization that we were going to die on the mountainside. And then a black well opened under me, and I fell into it.

When I came to in the morning, I discovered a well-made splint on my ankle, logs on the fire, and the smell of porridge cooking. I sat up and fire shot up my leg, and I groaned. Toren turned from the fire, his red-rimmed eyes telling me that he hadn't slept all night. But something was wrong, and with a sudden shock, I remembered that we were in my cave.

None of the workbenches had been disturbed, but he had opened my caches in search of something. I could explain this, I thought... and then I remembered that I had set my crook aflame, and there was no denying what I was.

He saw me stir, and said, "Good thing you had some sturdy wood here, so that I could make the splint. It was a clean break, so if you keep off it, you should be healed by the time the snows melt."

"By the time the snows melt? That'll be weeks."

"You are lucky to be alive," he said, with steel in his voice, "so were I in your position, I would not complain about a little enforced inactivity."

"Were I in *your* position," I replied, "I wouldn't have tried to play goddamned hero. I wouldn't have gone out into the storm after those sheep in the first place!"

"They were my responsibility to keep, and I let them go. I failed, and I tried to repair my mistake," he said, color rising to his cheeks.

"Toren, they were just sheep! They'll be a hard loss, sure, but they were lost when you left the mountain. No getting them back. You understand? Sometimes you have to let go."

He opened his mouth to reply, and I cut him off. "What's more, in addition to the hardship of losing those animals, in addition to my dead sheep, Inger's dead, too, my ankle's bust, and you don't have nearly the skill to handle the whole flock, not with a single dog, not with a pack of dogs, because you're too goddamned proud to give up a sheep. I'd think that a *military man*," and I said these words with my temper rising behind the pain in my ankle, the uneducated cadences of the life I'd chosen slipping away in my natural voice, "a *military man* would know when a battle's not worth fighting, but apparently you think that because you've seen war and maybe commanded a few men that shepherding is an all-or-nothing job. Well, guess what, Toren? It's not! Sometimes we have to make sacrifices, too, and if you can't remember that, then you're doomed in any job you take. If we're going to bring this flock through the winter, we're going to need help. More to the point, *you're* going to need help. I know you're worried about your secrecy—"

"My secrecy? *My secrecy?* Says the shepherd who turns out to be a magus! It's a fine wizard's tower you've got here, though perhaps I'd be better served by calling it a burrow!"

I retorted, "Perhaps it's because the people you hide from would crush me just as readily! Have you ever considered that you're not the only person who has enemies would see them dead?"

He leaned forward, eyes gleaming. "Oh, and now we get to it. What's your allegiance? Do you pledge fealty to any of the High Houses, or the Lesser?"

"Don't be ridiculous," I snapped. "My allegiance is to those poor farmers out there, the shepherds and the merchants. I saw what the Houses do when Amchester exploded. I see it every day when Farthington's men come and press another soul or two into service. I saw it in the service of the old Archmagus, and in that of her disciple, and on the battlefields from which they took their corpses for research. Don't talk to me about the Houses." If he was an Imperial agent, I reflected, I was dead anyway. Might as well get my real feelings out. I spat for good measure, and it was if the intervening years had vanished—my mind was with me, and I was the equal of any man in this province.

His eyes pinned mine, like he wanted to search my soul with them. I held his gaze steady. I'd held far worse. Obviously, he was deciding how far he could trust me.

"Don't be a fool," I said. "Do you really think your enemies put me out here in the off chance that you might happen by? Do you really think that my *burrow* is a spy's hideout? If I were in the employ of Terona, you can bet that I'd be living a damn sight more comfortably than this. And I'd have a farspeaker here, too. But I see that you've searched the place and haven't found anything, so..." I trailed off, losing my fire, "...so there's that."

"Fine," he said. "Fine." A formal tone crept into his voice. "First, I must express my gratitude for your hospitality, and then I must apologize for telling you the truth now. When they come after me, you must answer them as honestly as possible so that they do not put you too harshly to the question. I am Tomas Glasyin, formerly commander of the Imperial armed forces, duke of someplace I am no longer welcome, and so forth. I am in hiding from Terona, where my friend the king is about to die, and I can do nothing to save him. Now... who are *you?*"

I looked around my cave, and said, "I was found, amnesiac, in the ruins of Amchester. They sent me to Askelath to recover, in care of Westkitt Abbey. They taught me the scriptures and trained me in the ways of the hawk and dove, and at night they strapped me to a chair and ran lightning across my skull. To restore my memory, they said, but they kept to it even as my memories returned, and I could hear their disappointment that whatever they were doing wasn't working. I clamped down on some of my memories, never let them out." I chose these next words carefully, chewed them out one at a time, knowing the effect they'd have on this soldier. "I never told them that my parents had been agents of the Cronen, and that they died as they laid the explosives that took the Empire to war with the Siullan Republic."

He surged to his feet, horrified and ready to strike at something, anything, and I could not keep my scorn from my voice. "Really? Did you really think the Siullans did that? Did you honestly never think of the benefits that accrued to the High Houses and the Empire because of that incident?

The Empire gained all of the Siullan Republic. Their men garrison our southern and northern borders now. Their trade flows into our coffers. And their magic!"

He sat back, suddenly a-tremble, and I continued, stabbing my finger to accentuate my point. "Oh, yes. After the Westkitts decided I was useless to them but still showed remarkable mental prowess, they sent me off to the Council of Magi for training, and I learned well. I had access to the council's researches. The Siullans had advanced considerably in certain avenues: explosives, for instance. If an impartial and knowledgeable observer had actually looked at the Amchester blast, they'd have recognized it as far too primitive for the Siullans' work."

Numbly, he said, "So you're the son of traitors and destroyers."

"No," I replied. "I'm the son of patriots. They thought they were doing a service to their masters, but they also thought they would be able retire from the money they'd be paid. They were fooled, and they were *certainly* paid for their trouble. Think about it, Toren... I'm sorry, Tomas: Have the High Houses ever hesitated at anything to grasp more power for themselves? How many battles have they fought with each other? How much common blood have they spilled so that their sons and daughters remain fat and happy? How much blood have *you* spilled in their names, upholding their laws? Look at the villages around here. Would you say they've been well served by the Empire?"

"They receive protection... from the reavers, from the warlords, from..." He cradled his head in his hands. "From us. They pay us so we don't hurt them. And then we hurt them anyway."

"I know this is a shock," I said. "But out here, where the Houses rule mostly in name, we see things much differently than they do in Terona. We see the effects of their policies, and we suffer accordingly. When I finished my apprenticeship in the magi, they sent me against a tower in the south to claim it for myself against the other candidates. I refused to fight, and they stripped me of my staff. They declared my life forfeit, and they prepared an execution for me. But I still had friends, and my friends helped me burn a hole in my cell, and I fled here. Now you know why I hide. Now you know why I hate."

He looked up at last. "I have spent my life supporting Terona's order.

I have crushed rebellions. I have used the armies of the Empire to enforce peace within and without its borders. I have killed our citizens in the name of the king. You must hate everything I stand for."

"*Stood* for," I corrected. "Are you not an outcast? You haven't done any more than anyone else has done. You did what my parents did. You had no reason to question your life. It had meaning, purpose, and comfort, so why should you have cared?"

"I never thought..." He did not finish his sentence. "I should go. I have been a poor friend and a poor citizen." He stood.

As he staggered toward the cave mouth, I thought about the sheep he'd cost me, and about the broken bone that would likely not heal right for however many years I had left. I thought about these things, and then I set them aside. I said, "No. Don't go. It'd be a shame to throw away the one good friend I've had in these past twenty years just so I could get back to being lonely for the few years left before I die. At least now we can be honest with each other, eh?"

He came back and knelt before me, clasped my hand with both of his. "I need to evaluate my life. Everything you say... I could ignore it, but these last few months have turned all I know around. What are the chances that the two of us would meet here, this far from Terona?"

"Why," I said, "it's not so difficult to believe. This is at the far reaches of the Empire, on the edges of the Sickened Lands. This is almost a logical place for outcasts, exiles, and rebels."

He said, "I'll run the sheep myself until you've healed."

"And lose still more?"

"I won't lose more."

"Yes, you will. You can't handle the whole flock, Toren... Tomas! No, I'll just keep calling you Toren. It's easier. Now look: I've watched you with 'em. Listen to me. You need help. Further, I need the town's doctor, because you might be able to battle-dress a broken bone, but I'll be damned if I'll trust this without a second pair of eyes on it. We'll get back to the cottage, and from there, you'll need to go to the town pub, and they'll tell you where to find her. If Paul Busmith's there—a youngish man, strong looking, brown hair—

see if he's free to help you 'til my ankle's healed. He's a good lad. Hard worker." I struggled to my feet, and he stepped forward to help me rise.

We stepped out into the fresh snow. I heard him call Crosh to him, and we struggled back, saving our breath for the walk through the snow. It must have dropped at least two feet overnight, and when we made it to the cottage, I collapsed onto my bunk and woke only when Toren came back with Synor Vedru, a learned woman from the high alpine deserts of southern Haramai. What brought her to Dunlop I couldn't say, but she was quiet, and though we'd spoken a number of times, we weren't close friends. I don't know anyone who knew her well, but the woman was the best doctor we'd had in these parts for all the time I'd been here. She had a sharp eye and a sharp mind, and I was always sure to keep my little projects hidden away when I knew she'd be coming to call.

Vedru came in, skipped the small talk, and got straight to examining my ankle. After a few minutes of examination, she placed my staff in my hand, slipped a leather strip through my jaws, and said, "Hold him." Toren put one hand on my chest, the other on my leg, and leaned down on me. I bit hard on the leather strap, clutched the staff harder, and the doctor did something that made the day go away for a little while.

When I opened my eyes, she was done, and she was giving Toren instructions on my care. She looked over, saw me awake, and said, "I am leaving you a small bottle of syrup. You may take two drops from it every four hours, if the pain is bad. More than that will give you dreams, and the dreams will make you desire more until you can think of nothing else, and your life will be ruined. More than that will kill you. Two drops, four hours. No more."

She nodded her head to both of us and was off into the day, the sun streaming in bright off the fallen snow outside. When the door closed behind her, I said, "Was Paul there?"

"Yes, he was. He'll be by later today to help. He seems a bright enough lad, and not nearly as inquisitive as some of the townsfolk."

"What do you mean?"

"I've faced lighter questioning from guards on a picket line," he said.

"Who am I, where'd I come from, how'd you hire me on, and how'd you happen to break your ankle. I told them as little as I could, but these farmers are tenacious."

"Yep. How're the sheep?"

"I've fed them twice today at the troughs, but they won't go out into the snow."

"No, I suppose they wouldn't for you. Here's what you do..." and we fell into a discussion of the care of sheep in winter, interrupted by the arrival of Paul an hour or so later.

The lad nodded to us quietly, came over, and knelt by my bedside. "Paul, Toren here has been to the cave. He knows. I trust him, and you can, too. Do what you can to hide the evidence of our work there until I'm able to get back. There's no point in continuing unless I'm there to supervise."

When I finished, Paul told me he understood, and gestured Toren to the door.

Toren said, "If you need anything, call out, all right?"

"You won't hear me, Toren. You're going too far for that. I'll be fine."

They left, and I stared at the ceiling for some time before heaving myself from bed with the aid of my staff. I sat dozing by the fire, waiting for evening to come, and let my mind wander through the various plans I'd laid, and at some point I fell asleep.

After the two came back that night and Paul returned to his cottage, Toren sat with me for a bit quietly, both of us in chairs in front of the fire. After a few minutes, he spoke.

"I've had time to think," he said. "And I'm going to stay. I've no purpose now, but if you'll have me, I'll stay. I don't know what you're making there or what you're doing in your cave, and I don't want to know. Not right now. But in time, I might want to help. Will you have me?"

"Better with us than against us, sir."

He grinned with relief and leaned back into his chair. The firelight danced on his face.

After that day, we established a new routine: Paul arrived in the morning, he and Toren fed the sheep and cleaned the barn so the sheep runoff didn't turn noxious, and as the snow melted, started taking them out to the pastures. Paul went up to the eastern hills, leaving Toren with the usual western spots. Toren knew to fetch the boy if anything went amiss. And me, I stayed indoors with the fire and let my mind wander. It stayed this way until the snows melted in two months, and I was able to hobble out to the barn with the aid of my staff.

At last, as spring was in full flower, Vedru came by and told me that I was allowed to do work in the immediate area, but to leave the long walks for the other men for at least another month or two. But Paul told me that Toren was likely able to handle the flock by himself, and so I let the boy get back to his pursuits. Once he'd finished stowing the gear, there was nothing I really needed to look after in my caves right now.

That same day, as I stood winded atop the small hill near my cottage, my leg afire from my exertions and sweat running into my eyes, I looked down on the main road and saw a pair of riders on gray horses galloping at top speed toward Dunlop. I caught my breath and limped carefully down the hill to my cottage. I was there for perhaps thirty minutes when Paul came tearing to my door. I rose from my sturdy old chair to greet him, but he waved me down, caught his breath, and gasped. When at last he could breathe, he said, "The king's been attacked!"

"What happened? Do you know?" I had expected this day since Glasyin had revealed himself.

"Two post riders came to town on horses near dead, told the mayor the news, and tore south on fresh horses from the post."

"How did it happen?"

"Mayor says that it was one of the King's Chosen who did it." His voice was awed and quiet.

"Did they catch the one responsible?"

"No. They say he slaughtered the king's kids, escaped, and set Terona on fire before he left. The knighthood is looking for him, and they say that the magi are, too, and they'll be combing the country to find him. The queen fled the city, they say, and they don't know where she is either."

"Did they tell the mayor who's going to rule now?"

"I heard that it was a duke. I don't remember his name. They said it was just until the king got better or they figured out the succession."

"Thank you, Paul."

He left, and I sat and massaged my leg and stared into the fire and thought dark thoughts about the projects I had brewing in my sheds and how that work looked like it had all gone to waste now.

When Toren put the sheep in that night, I made my way to the barn and said, "Nice day out today, aye?"

"Nice enough, I'd say. The snow has melted from the pastures, and the fields are coming in well."

"Think the sheep are ready to leave the barn for forage?"

"I'd think so."

"Good, good. Toren, have a seat. You'll want to sit."

His face closed, guarded, he sat. "Yes?"

"You claimed the king as your friend, some months ago. News today has it that he has been severely wounded."

It had been a long time since I'd seen someone keep such perfect control. His voice and hands shook only slightly as he said, "How?"

"One of the King's Chosen, they say. The queen has disappeared, and one of the nobles is claiming the crown... temporarily, of course, to keep order." I don't think I was successful in keeping the cynicism out my voice, but I don't think he noticed.

"So it's started," he said. "We should be on the watch for assassins. If they had the audacity to kill the king, what paltry thing would it be for them to come for me?"

"I said wounded, not dead. And who is *they*? I said it was one of the King's Chosen who did it, not a group of them."

The look he turned on me was pitying. "This is a conspiracy, and the conspirators will be rewarded with an empire. I think he's dead, and they're holding the announcement to let Duke Athedon settle comfortably into the regency, to preserve appearances. If the king isn't dead, it's only because they need to show him to the crowd and let him name his successor publicly. Maybe they've got the queen someplace as a hostage for his good behavior. But no. No, I think he's dead, and Terona will never see his face again. So I'll be staying here, I think. I'm not done learning this shepherd trade yet. And you know, I think I'd like to know more about what you're doing in those caves."

"But—"

"Dark times are about to come to us, Ysabel. Lawless times. We may be seeing the end of everything we know. I don't see any hope now."

I didn't know what to say to that, so I just nodded and backed out the door. As I closed the door behind me, I heard him mutter, "You didn't have to kill him, you bastards. He was nearly dead already."

I watched the barn door from the cottage, and he didn't come out for more than an hour, after the sun had set.

I didn't expect to see him the next morning, and I admit I gave a start of surprise when he came right on time. He didn't look like he'd slept much. I gave him a nod, and he nodded back, and we got back to the routine, but I watched him walk up the western slope, and he walked like he'd been kicked in the gut. I wondered how close he was to old Fannon, and how much his life was worth now—and I suppose he had been wondering the same thing.

When he came back down the hill that evening, it seemed he'd come to peace with it. I didn't say anything to him about it. I figured he'd start talking when he was ready. But he never did, and he never left. He just got quieter, more withdrawn, and he stayed that way into summer. I tried to engage him about the project, but it was no use. It was like he was giving up. It wasn't until Midsummer's Eve that I saw him change.

Toren was already off to the hills that morning when there came a knock on my door. I opened it to find a dark young man on my doorstep. He wore a backpack over his rough clothes, and I could see a head of dark hair peeking from over his shoulder—the backpack was a sling, then, for his child. An itinerant father, I thought, a beggar looking for scraps for his child. Hard to believe a face that proud and hard could stoop to begging, but I'd seen stranger things in my time.

"I've got some crusts and milk, if you'll have it," I said, "but I've got no money, nor do I have work for pay."

"I'm not looking for coin nor scraps," he said, his voice flat. "I've heard that there are two old shepherds here, and you're not the one I'm looking for. Where is the other?"

"Toren?" I said. "He's with the flock, but he..." and it was then that I looked at him closely, saw his scars and the strength in his arms. "Who are you?"

"A mendicant. That is all you need to know for now. Save me the trouble of tracking him across these valleys. It will not improve my temper toward you if I have to hunt for him. You cannot send a message to him before I reach him, you have no dog here to fetch him, you have no falcons or pigeons to warn him, and your fire is only ashes. I mean him no harm, but if I did, you could not stop me, and I would wrench the answer from your skin and blood. So tell me: where does he pasture?"

Something dark in that intensely weary face convinced me that I shouldn't delay. "He's in the west pasture. Take the small road past the front gate to where it forks around the central hill, and go west. He'll be on the slopes of Eagle Rock. Know that he'll be able to spot you well before you see him. He knows me, he knows the townsfolk, and when he sees you coming, he will be long gone."

"Though he does not know it yet, he will want to see me. I have traveled long to find him." He pulled his hand from the door and turned quick on his heel. I closed the door behind him and hobbled for my crook. Though I am old, though I fled rather than fight another magus, that young man wasn't capable of anything but evil, it seemed to me, and now seemed a fine time to break my spell of cowardice.

As I reached the door, ready to call fires with my crook and set the man ablaze, I could see the stranger passing through the meadows, moving faster on his feet than any normal man had a right to do. And that's when it all clicked together for me—this wasn't any normal man. This was one of the King's Chosen. Was this the man who tried assassinate the king? Even if Toren fled from here, there was no eluding one of these bloodhounds, and the young man with the dead eyes had likely come to kill one of the last parts of the old regime to complete the conspiracy in Terona. He'd come to kill my friend. But I might be able to stop him before he could. Even the knights fall before magic.

I left my house as quick as I could run, hurried as fast as I could up the western slope. I don't know what I was hoping to accomplish—maybe to give Toren enough warning to hide or set up an ambush, or even (dared I hope) to bring the killer down. Fitting that he'd die in flame, this arsonist of Terona.

For some reason, at no point did I wonder why the boy was traveling with a baby.

I rushed across the open ground, each step sending a small shock up my healing leg, and cursed my age again and again. The earth itself seemed ready to trip me up—my staff caught in rabbit holes, small pebbles turned large under my foot, my cloak caught in the bushes and thistles. I was breathing hard, the sweat standing out on my forehead, and a dim despair came over me as I realized I'd be lucky even to get within shouting range. Halfway to the pasturing lands, a great pain exploded in my ankle, and I pitched forward onto my face.

I clawed my way up, spitting dirt, and realized that my only chance in warning Toren lay in my staff. I took the deepest breath my old lungs could swallow, bit my lip, and levered myself to my feet. I blazed my staff into the sky, launching a flaming bolt a hundred feet into the air, its explosion echoing on the hills. I shouted, "Toren! Run!"

And it was only then that I realized that maybe Dunlop could see that bolt as well. Now I was going to have to come up with a story. I sat back down and tore a strip from my cloak, wrapped it tight around my ankle, and began to hobble back down toward my house. I had to formulate something that'd keep people from talking about this, or figure out a way to make it look like something else. Curse the gods to a piss-soaked hell! If the Council sent a magus to investigate, I'd be found for sure. Likewise, if the knight came back to finish me off after he'd killed my friend, I'd want to have something ready for him. When I returned, I splinted my ankle (again!), finished my preparations, and then sat facing the door, my staff laid across my lap, and waited.

I heard the complaints of bleating of the sheep, and I straightened myself in my chair, ready to trigger my surprises. But the tone of the voices that intermingled with the bleating was wrong. I recognized the slight lilt of Toren's northern accent and the flat affect of the knight, and Toren sounded... glad?

I stood quickly and disarmed the traps and opened the door to Toren's smiling face, and the face of the kingslayer.

Toren smiled slightly and said, "Ysabel, it is my great pleasure to present you to Her Royal Highness, Princess Caitrona, and her guardian, Sir Pelagir Amons of the Knights Elite."

I sat right back down, my mouth hanging open, and the killer stepped into my house, cradling the baby as if it were his own.

Toren said, "The sheep are in the barn. Crosh is watching them for these few moments. Let me put some food together, and I'll explain what I can."

When they'd found a seat, Toren sat in front of me and examined my outstretched leg. "When you said that this was a logical place for outcasts and rebels, my friend, I did not think the implications through. The fact that Pelagir could find me within months of my arrival has shown me that I am most certainly not safe remaining here."

"Did you see my warning signal?" I asked.

"I did, and if you'll forgive me, that's another reason I must leave. You have been here for years, and may be able to explain that. But I am new, and Pelagir and the princess are newer still, and so we must leave. Now.

Our presence here endangers you as well."

I rose and hobbled to the kitchen. "In that case, let me speed you on your way. You'll need food and drink, fresh clothing, and money. I do not have much, but—"

Pelagir handed me five gold coins, more than I'd seen in one place in years. "Take this. I have more."

"Sir Pelagir tells me," Toren continued, "that he took no part in the king's death."

"I thought the king merely wounded," I said.

"No," said Pelagir. "He was to have been killed that night, and some few exceptions aside," he glanced at the old general, "the conspirators did not generally fail in their tasks."

"Toren, do you believe him?" I asked, looking at that dark, impassive face.

"Without reserve. He has been cruelly used by those who had his trust, and furthermore, he has held my life in his hands and gave it back to me. He had the courage to do what I could not, acting against the conspirators when none else would. Pelagir, tell him what happened."

The young man spoke: "Duke Athedon—the man who has now taken the throne—approached me, and spoke to me of honor and duty. He spoke to me of gratitude, and bade me listen to the king and his advisors, and how they appreciate the mortal service their subjects tender them. Not three days later, as I stood guard outside His Majesty's chamber, I heard him speak to the queen about our lack of ambition, our willingness to be slaughtered for his whim, and he laughed. He *laughed* at our sacrifice, and I thought then that he was unworthy of our devotion. I sought out the duke and asked him what he planned."

"Was the queen a part of the plot?"

"Absolutely not," said Pelagir. "Would she have willingly removed herself from power? She would not have been able to secure an alliance with the Cronen, and no matter her personal faults, she would not have seen her children murdered for her gain."

"Very well. What did the duke say when you questioned him about this?" I asked.

"He said that he wished to restore honor to the Empire and to the knighthood, to bring back the glory that had been squandered under Fannon and his family. He told me that he scoffed at us for the queen's sake, so that she would consider us beneath her notice, and I believed him. Even then I trusted him. He drew me into his confidence, just enough that I would feel myself to be an integral part of his plot, and so I was. I was to be the scapegoat. It was early spring, months after the general fled because he could do nothing to stop this betrayal." He nodded respectfully at Toren, who interjected.

"I tried, dammit! Not one of my compatriots proved worthy of my trust!"

Pelagir held up a placatory hand. "Nothing could have changed the course of events, sir. The duke approached you as a formality. You were a piece of the puzzle, but not integral. As long as he could take the army, he did not need you except as a figurehead."

Toren nodded, half-mollified.

Pelagir continued his story. "I followed one of the duke's compatriots, a duchess, one night to a meeting I was to attend later. I listened as he and she spoke of their allies in the knighthood, and their dupe who would take the blame. And it was then that I discovered that Duke Athedon intended not to glorify the knights, but eliminate us altogether and form a new force that would be entirely loyal to him and his family, rather than to the Empire."

"I tried to warn my captain of this, and when he tried to have me killed outside his chambers, I discovered that he was a part of the conspiracy. I escaped, killing two of my brethren. I went to the nursery and slew the assassin there before taking one of the children; I could carry no more and still effect an escape. I left through the kitchens, arrived in the stable, found my courser and destroyed another by overloading the core in its chest so that it exploded, leaving the keep burning behind me. I came west, seeking the one man whose leadership may save us. There are others I trust, but they are not leaders of his caliber."

"How did you find him here, far from Terona?"

"I am one of the Knights Elite," he said, as if that answered the question.

Toren said, "They have blamed Pelagir for the king's death, as we have heard, and so we must assume that they are moving ahead with their plan to discredit the knighthood. What Pelagir has accomplished is the salvation of the royal family, though what good it will do us now remains to be seen. At any rate, we should be moving."

"Of course." We rose, and I whistled Crosh to round up the sheep. We began walking back toward the cottage. Pelagir moved quickly, instinctively, his long strides eating up the ground, and he slowed down only with a visible effort. "Before you go, Pelagir, I have a question."

"What is it?"

"Toren knows about the caves, but perhaps you do not. I received some training as a magus, but I fled Terona in disgrace years ago. I've had some time to put together a few odds and ends that you might find useful, and I've had the help of a few townsfolk who're sick of being stepped on by the powerful. They'd help you if you'd help them. Give me the word and we'll put my work to use."

"No," he said.

My friend Toren added, "The time isn't right, and these shepherds and townsfolk will be slaughtered if they try anything. The army will strike hard at trouble spots during the transition and will make severe examples of those who think to take advantage of this time. No. Continue with your livelihood, teach the children, train them quietly, and if we can manage it, someone will return to check on your progress."

"All right," I said. "I can't say I'm not disappointed. So nothing now?"

"Not if you value your life. And not if you intend for your revolt to have a chance at success."

"Fine," I said, but I was thinking differently. "What are your plans?"

"I can't tell you that." He looked carefully at me. "It's best you not know, both for your sake and for ours. It is one thing that you know our names.

It is another thing altogether to know our plans."

"You'd best be going, then. No time to waste." I grinned. "I'll try to restrain myself."

Pelagir stood out in the yard already, the girl on his back, looking around alertly. Toren—Glasyin—took my hands in his and said, "I wish we could have brought something better to you, and if we come through this alive, I'll see to it that you're handsomely repaid."

"We'll see," I said. "Who knows what'll happen?"

I had packed food enough for several days, and I bade them farewell from my yard. I stood and watched them walk north, the young knight carrying the princess and the pack, the general—my last true friend—walking alongside. I watched until they were out of sight, and then I went back to explain the fire in the sky.

Epilogue: Into the North

Midsummer, CY 586

The two travelers and their child traveled the road, drawing discreetly to the side whenever carriages or post riders thundered past them. They soon wore a coat of mud despite their care, and it was only the quick reactions of the younger man that kept the face of the baby girl he carried from being spattered as well.

He watched the older man from the corner of his eye as they walked, but then his eyes roamed everywhere even as the rest of him seemed to be at peace. At last, the older man sighed and leaned on his staff.

"You have something to say, Sir Knight. You've been waiting to say it since we left the farm, and you're trying to find a way to broach the subject gracefully. Well, then. We're not at court anymore. You have betrayed your oath"—the young knight flinched visibly at this—"so you might as well come to terms with it. I suspect you have hardly been thinking of the issue, intent on your mission of finding me or dancing around it, but you should let it sink in. You have betrayed your oath to your country, and you are traveling in the company of an exile from the court, an old general likely labeled a traitor and with a price on his head. I think it's best that we speak honestly with each other, rather than spare the other's feelings."

Pelagir searched Glasyin's face. "Very well, General. What I wanted to—"

"No," said Glasyin. "Call me Toren. Not Glasyin. Not lord. Not general. Get out of those habits now. They will kill us if uttered in the wrong ears. You can still call me sir if it will make you feel better."

"Yes, sir."

"Better. Now what was your question?"

The youth swallowed. "I had not thought past finding you, sir. I am trained to fight and kill. I have studied tactics and strategy. I have read how to build an insurgency. But I don't know how to raise a child, and I don't know what to do next."

"So you're looking for a commanding officer to push you in the right direction?"

"Yes, sir. I have spent my life taking commands. I need to serve under someone I can trust."

Glasyin sighed, and said, "All right. Our first job is deception. We must become new people. With times being what they are and the nobles going at each other, it's easy enough. We can be refugees looking for a new home. Since I don't think you can lose the habit of calling me 'sir,' you will have been recently discharged from the army. I am your grandfather, Toren. You are my grandson, and your name is . . . what's your mother's name?"

"Arulia, sir."

"Your name is Arul now."

"Yes . . . grandfather."

Glasyin—Toren—coughed. "I think 'sir' sounds better from your mouth."

"Yes, sir. But what about Her Highness?"

"What about her?"

"She needs a name. And who shall we entrust to raise her properly?"

A sharp look. "Entrust? No one. We do it ourselves."

"We, sir? Have you ever raised a child?"

The old man smiled thinly. "Your father. And you, when he died. We need to remember this. And now I'm helping you raise your daughter, because your wife died in the attack on our village. It needs to be a northern village. Let's choose Half-crest. It's far enough away that no one will send for our information. Have you ever been there?"

"Sir, I meant in your real life."

"This is my real life now. Boy, I don't like this any better than you, but we're going to have to accept our current circumstances. Whether we do a good job with her depends entirely on what our goals are. I've seen enough of the spoiled nobility to know that our little princess will be better off being raised outside Terona. She might not have the courtly graces, but we can make her honest."

"When do we restore her to the throne? And how?"

"Sir Kn . . . Arul, I have barely had time to think about that. By the time she's ready, it might very well be the case that there's no empire left for her to rule. Fortunately, we have time to think that over. What we don't have is a place to live, and that's our most pressing issue. You still have money, I saw."

"I do."

Glasyin said, "Then our first business is to find ourselves horses, and then find ourselves a home near a place with books. What sorts of skills do you have besides fighting?"

"Frankly, sir, not many."

"Any farm work?"

"No, sir. My father was a Knight Faithful."

"All right. So we're a military family, and that explains why we're so piss-poor at this work. I can do some shepherding, you can apprentice yourself out to a smith. We can't draw attention to ourselves more than necessary. We need to fade in fast and stay out of trouble, get into the fabric of the town quickly enough that they forget about us. That means we need to find a place where it's not so tight-knit that we'll be all they talk about. And that means we need a town of about a thousand people or more.

"Fortunately," he said, "I made a study of the towns about a hundred miles around this area during my official duties, and I have an idea where we can go. It's a small town called Kingsecret. Martyn's heirs used it as a retreat from Terona, and then it was overrun with nobility, and then they all abandoned it. Most of the mansions have been torn down and replaced, and while there are a few noble bastards with the run of the place, the Imperial spies have mostly decided that it's not worth keeping a serious eye on it."

Glasyin looked at the ground, thinking. "Of course, I have no true idea where the spies are these days. But then, we take a chance everywhere we go."

Pelagir thought for a moment and nodded. "Agreed. Another question: What shall we tell her of her past?"

"Nothing. At least, not until she's old enough to understand. We'll talk about her lessons as the time comes, but she should be well educated."

Pelagir considered this and began to number them on his fingers. "Skill at arms. Command, strategy, and tactics. History of the Empire. History of the Houses. History of our foreign neighbors. Ecclesiastical studies. Economics. The great philo—"

"Enough! Perhaps we should focus on reading and writing first. Keep in mind that by the time she is old enough to study these things, I will be even older. I may suffer dementia. I have seen it happen to younger men. You must study as well so that you can step in to take over when I die."

"I cannot teach—"

Glasyin snapped, "If you cannot teach her, why did you take her? Who else will be responsible? As much as you may admire me for my refusal to betray my friend, your admiration will not stop the march of time. I am not a young man. Accept that."

That night, as they sat before the campfire, Glasyin was struck by a thought. "Tell me: Have you rid yourself of all the trackers they might use to find you?"

"I left my sword and horse in Westport before I boarded the ship."

Glasyin studied him, stroking the beard he had grown over the long winter. "I wonder if the magi's gift might be something deeper than your blade and your steed."

Pelagir stared at Glasyin for a moment and said, "Yes. Perhaps. During the Battle of Malaqin, a sinkhole swallowed Commander Carderas, and none saw where he had vanished. His weapon and courser were near his headquarters, but the captain knew where to dig to retrieve him."

"Well. This complicates matters. We need to see an old friend of mine. I don't think you'll care for him. His name is Underhill."

And so they came to the town of Lower Pippen, where the old man made inquiries in a certain tavern. That night, they were met by a man outside town, and they slept in his strange, sun-seeking tower for a month. For a day, the basement of the tower echoed with groans of agony and occasionally a powerful roar. Pelagir remained in bed for a week thereafter, swathed in bandages. Glasyin watched the baby in this time, and she began to love him in the unconditional way that babies love anyone who treats them well. When at last Pelagir rose, he walked unsteadily, and the old man and the magus spoke quietly with each other.

At last, the three travelers set out again. They traveled alone, except when it would look suspicious for them to avoid company. Slowly, over the weeks it took them to reach Kingsecret, Pelagir began to lose his stiff and formal manner, though he continued to speak from a well of deep reserve.

Months later, in the small hill-town of Kingsecret, an old man, a young man, and his daughter bought a struggling sheep farm, the old man counting out the silver as if it were his last hope. The farmhouse was built into the hillside, and the new family improved it by building terraces and a garden, and if there wasn't always evidence of digging outside to explain the dirt piles that sometimes appeared, no one made any mention of it. If any villagers had gone to investigate, they would have found that the young man was expanding the farmhouse by turning it into an underhill fortress past a hidden door.

The young man took himself to the blacksmith and began to learn the trade, and although he was far too old for ordinary apprenticing, he took quickly to the work. His powerful, scarred arms invited comment; his face did not. He deflected questions about his past genially but firmly, and the people of the town assumed that he had seen horrors in the wars. The newcomers found a wet nurse for the baby, and the travelers faded into the background—just friendly enough and open enough to ease suspicion, but not so gregarious that any would have called them friends.

Occasionally the young man would take journeys to the nearby city of Avollan and return with a donkey laden down with supplies: hardware, books, writing utensils. He had grown a beard and favored wide-brimmed hats when he left town.

The baby began to crawl, walk, and talk. She was possessed of a natural grace and charm but could generate truly powerful rages when thwarted. She spent most of her time with her family, learning how to watch the sheep with her da and listening to his stories with wide eyes.

And time passed.

Colonies and protectorates of the Empire felt their leashes slipping and began to revolt. Old enemies raised their heads. Conscriptions took farmers from their fields and merchants from their trades; the smith and his apprentice were careful to watch for press gangs in towns and on the road. There were food shortages and riots in the cities as the fields turned wild; with the farmers gone, the fields went unharvested.

The unreliable stories from the roads had the Houses at one another's throats, the Birdsnest Wars come again in blood and pain. Duke Athedon the regent instituted martial law in some of the lesser cities and colonies and brought the rebel leaders to Terona for public trials and painful executions. A wave of assassinations swept through lower ranks of the Houses, and some of the more tractable nobles fell in line behind Athedon.

Slowly, very slowly, Athedon began to exert control. With his allies in the Council of Magi, the Council of Knights, and the High Exegetes of the Church, he consolidated his strength. And even in the far-flung provinces, the citizens of the Empire could feel his fingers around their throats, and they shivered in the chill of the growing shadow.

END OF PART ONE

Acknowledgements

This is the part where I get to thank everyone without whose help I could not have done even this much. Naturally, all errors are mine. Any advice or insight provided to me was done so on the basis of expertise and authority, and I converted it for use in developing the story. If I have destroyed details, forgotten something, or bastardized that knowledge, it is entirely my responsibility and no blame should accrue to others.

Many thanks to those who worked on this book. It is good to know people, but in particular, it is very, very good to know these people.
- My editor, Ray Vallese, who needs no adjective because he is superlative.
- My fantastic cover artist, Stone Perales (www.stonewurks.com)
- Graphic designer extraordinaire, Don Strandell (www.donstrandell.com)
- Electronic formatting maestro, game designer, and writer Guido Henkel (www.guidohenkel.com)
- Andrew Hernandez, for suggestions, advice, and help of all stripes.

To my first readers: Bradford Clay Matheson, Gavin and Scott McComb, Kevin Pohle (and Toni and Andrew and Nickel), David Thomas, and David Wise. Your insights and enthusiasm kept me going.

For invaluable advice, whether they knew they were giving it or not: Phil Athans, my brother Mike McComb of the US Navy, and Pierce Watters.

For some particular friends, who helped spark my brain: Chris Avellone, who is dreamy; Chip Bumgardner, who is fearless; Monte Cook, who taught me to yes, have some; Bruce Cordell, leader of Team Ninja; Tony, Angela, and Sophia DiTerlizzi for a friendship almost two decades long; Paul and Jen Kemp and their three rapscallions (can I say rapscallions? Awesome); Sean Reynolds for being shavey first; and Steven Schend and Sarah Joseph and young Oscar, who is soon to be a big brother.

Many thanks to my patrons, both the ridiculously generous and the very interested. You know who you are. Your aid, no matter the amount, was humbling and uplifting. It is my sincere hope that you feel you've received fair value for your faith, and that you'll stick around to see where the story goes. Without you, this book might well have remained unpublished and unpolished.

To my senior patrons: Clinton J. Boomer, Will Cronenwett, Steven Dengler, and Nancy Wastcoat Garbett—enjoy your villainy!

To the faithful: Johnny Earle, Isabella McColi (the cat who made it possible), and Michelle Vuckovich, the original cool girl (now the cool woman).

To the players: Paul Buss (whose company I miss), my dearest sister Babbie Lester, my kindest brother Gavin McComb, Dick Olson who is venturing far from his comfort zone (brave soul!), and Michael Stoyanovich, with a perspective we should emulate.

To the fruitful: Amy Canaday and her delightful children, and to la familia Ortiz (Pablo, Mariela, Victoria, y Santiago), muchas mas gracias, and to Carrie Read (I'm still sorry about the F-word!), and to Aunt Polly Weissman.

To the readers: Paul Barrett, Jára Cervinka, Bruce Cordell, Brian Darnell, Uncle John and Aunt Babbie Earle, Nathan Filizzi, Scott Gable, Mary "Dr. Dream Chaser" Gebhart, Apollo Haner, Tracy Davis Hurley, Nicole Lindroos, Erik Lundqvist, Ben McFarland, Ryan Merlo (who is not a dick, no matter what Dan says), the vulture Danielle Radford, Steven Schend, Christopher Simokat, Aunt Wendy Sopkovich, Rob Steiner, Bradford Stephens, Val & Trevor & Delaney Vallese, and Aunt Connie Wastcoat and Don Strandell.

Thank you. Thank you all.

About the Author

Colin McComb was born in 1970 and began to read at the age of 4. At the age of 10 he began to game. At 12 he knew what he wanted to be. At 21, he began to write professionally, first for TSR, Inc., where he wrote adventures and created worlds for the *Advanced Dungeons & Dragons* roleplaying game, including the Birthright campaign setting and significant work on Planescape. It was this latter work that led him to California and Black Isle Studios, where he contributed to *Planescape: Torment,* consistently (and independently) voted as one of the best computer RPGs ever (if he does say so himself). He met his wife, the beautiful and talented Robin Moulder, and moved to Michigan in 2000. He has contributed to Paizo Publishing, Malhavoc Press, Open Design, and many more.

Colin is a member of two author collectives: the Alliterati and the Monumental Works Group (www.monumentalworksgroup.com).

Oathbreaker is his first published fiction.

www.ingramcontent.com/pod-product-compliance
Lightning Source LLC
Chambersburg PA
CBHW060635130626
46555CB00002B/810